The Seven Rings of Man's Destiny Book I:
Jimmy and the Azure Ring
By Tom Fricket

I0621477

The Seven Rings of Man's Destiny Book I:

Jimmy and the Azure Ring

Copyright © 2016 by Tom Fricket. All rights reserved.

ISBN: 978-0-9984260-0-6

To Tonya,

For your patience and support

Contents

Chapter One
The Secret Plan

It was a cool, Saturday morning in the month of October as Jimmy was opening his eyes to what he thought was just another ordinary day in Newford, Arkansas. He lay in bed for a few minutes, rubbing his eyes. He looked up at the ceiling at the poster of his favorite country singer, May Sting, who was donning a glittery diamond necklace and a dark blue blouse with long sleeves. She was also wearing air-tight, denim blue jeans. She was about as old as Jimmy when she was catapulted into stardom because of her uncanny voice range at such a young age. Jimmy liked her songs, specifically, "Two-Punch," and he thought she was gorgeous. Her poster helped him to wake up each morning with a smile to start his day.

After Jimmy had finished imagining himself with her by his side, he swung out of bed and to his feet. Today was the day that he and his best friend Ryan were to go spelunking in the cave they had discovered within the confines of a large land mass over in Riverside. But, first, he had to get ready. He and Ryan had planned this excursion for weeks, and they had somehow managed to keep quiet about it.

Jimmy grabbed his clothes and a towel out of the hall closet and headed for the bathroom to shower. He paused, as he always did before getting into the shower, to scan his face for weaknesses. He noticed a new zit that had formed on the lower left portion of his chin, so he decided to pop it. He wasn't particularly narcissistic about his appearance, but he didn't like acne and had struggled with it for months. His blue eyes and auburn hair stared back at him as he routinely brushed and flossed his teeth before showering each morning. He suited up for the day, wearing his baby-blue shirt, his camo pants, his new black, Nike Cross Tops and his brown, leather jacket. He loved wearing his leather jacket because he felt that it made him look dapper to the ladies.

Afterwards, Jimmy went into the kitchen as his mother was having coffee and his father was reading the newspaper, which was part of their morning routines. He opened one of the oak cabinets and reached for a box of Chocolate Bits, and he snatched a large, white bowl and a spoon from the dish drainer.

Jimmy's mother woke up at 6:15 each morning and made breakfast for them. She had been doing this for over a decade, though she slept until 9:00 on the weekends—and then it was every man for himself. She had been the Newford Junior High's secretary for just a shade under twelve years.

Jimmy's father, on the other hand, woke up at 6:30. He would usually shower first, and then he would go outside to get the newspaper. He read the paper and ate breakfast simultaneously. Jimmy often wondered how he accomplished this feat without dropping egg whites all over his khakis pants. He had been a tech coordinator for the entire Newford district for over fifteen years.

He also wondered why his father didn't read the news like everyone else: using a smartphone. After all, he was considered to be a technology guru, not to mention the fact that he insisted on having the most updated technology resources possible—as long as they were economical.

Unlike the many native hunters who were packing guns, his father was carrying the latest ePhone with a Cheetah processor that could calculate faster than a hundred bean counters. It was also adorned in a metallic material that could essentially stop the speeding bullets from those same guns. He, too, was packing heat—just with different specifications.

But, Jimmy also knew that his father was old-fashioned and believed in the adage: *If it's not broke, don't fix it,* which he tended to apply daily. Jimmy viewed his father as a paradox—a product of the past, but a patron of the future.

Jimmy sat down at the kitchen table with his large, white bowl of chocolate-flavored cereal. His mother, who was at one end, looked up from reading a news app on her oversized LS smartphone. Jimmy considered her phone a device for the elderly, though his mother was only forty-three.

"Good morning, J.R.," his mother said, being the first to notice that he had sat down at the kitchen table. J.R. stood for Jimmy Rood, but most people called him Jimmy, except for his father, who insisted on being set a part from his friends. His father, when appropriate, called him Jim because he felt that it was manly, and he believed it was his responsibility to teach him to become a man. "What do you have planned for your Saturday?" she asked, inquisitively.

"Oh, I thought I would stay the night with Ryan, if that's cool?" he replied, crunching away at his cereal and trying not to give away any details about his true intentions.

"I don't care, but you need to ask your father," she said, looking in his direction. Jimmy knew she didn't have to have his father's approval, but she would always refer to him out of respect.

"Dad—," he began.

"It's fine," his father stated abruptly, not looking up from the article he was reading. "I'll run you out there as soon as you finish your chores. I wanna talk to his mother about the new school app." He turned to the next page in the newspaper. "Why are we always into it with Russia?" he asked, reaching out for his cup of coffee with his left hand, while holding the paper in his lap with his right one.

Jimmy was amazed at his father's ability to process large amounts of information at once and come to a solid, distinctive decision. He speculated that this was why he was so good at his job.

"Cool, thanks," he replied, getting up from the table to put his bowl in the sink. Generally, Jimmy could do what he wanted on the weekends as long as his grades were good and his chores were done.

Jimmy couldn't wait for the day when he could drive his own vehicle. His father wouldn't let him drive his truck for more than a few miles at a time. Jimmy figured it was more about the truck being his own, and less about his father's trust in his driving abilities. He had his permit, but he was saving for a used, silver S20 pickup truck he had seen at one of the dealerships in Hillside Home, a nearby town. His parents made a deal with him: He had to save up half the money from his allowance, which about $80 a month, or he had to procure a job--which he wasn't old enough to have--and then his parents would match it. He calculated that, by his sixteenth birthday, he would have the amount he needed.

Once permission had been granted, Jimmy grabbed his new Ace 5 phone, went to his bedroom, and began texting Ryan.

To: Ryan;

Me: "What's up, dude, you ready for this thing. I hope you didn't tell anybody. You know you gotta big mouth lol."

Ryan: "No, man, I didn't tell anyone, dork. What time you comin'?"

Me: "'Bout 1:00, I guess, goober. I've got some chores to do first."

Ryan: "Aight, man, CYA—#wannabe player, BAG."

Me: "OK, dude--#Ryanthejackass, C&G."

After Jimmy finished cleaning his room and taking out the trash, his father drove him to Ryan's house in Riverside. On the way, his father began asking him questions about his choice of sleepover items.

"So, what are the two flashlights for, anyway?" he asked, curiously. *He must have seen me put them in my backpack. Be cool, Jimmy*, he thought to himself. "You guys going to camp out or something?" he asked, giving Jimmy the answer he needed.

"Uh, yeah, we thought we might camp out in Ryan's backyard," he lied quickly, so not to arouse any suspicions.

"We used to do that when I was your age. You may want to bring a sleeping bag next time, though," he suggested. His father was always reminding him about his childhood and the way he had done things growing up in Shideen, Arkansas.

"Oh, yeah, Ryan has everything already," he responded, cleverly. Normally, he enjoyed hearing about his father's childhood because it made him seem more human, but today he was trying to avoid these types of conversations. He knew that he wasn't very good at keeping secrets, and he was even worse at lying. He had a guilty conscience, but that wasn't the real concern. He really hated lying to his father.

As they pulled up into Ryan's driveway, Jimmy could see that Ryan was outside sitting on his porch, ready to greet them. Jimmy could make out his large grin from the passenger side window. He opened the door before the truck had come to a complete stop. He could feel his father's eyes on him and knew his head was shaking.

"What's up, goober? Did you bring the flashlights? I've got the sleeping bags, the snacks, the sodas, and the light sticks," he said, enthusiastically, moving his hands in different directions to emphasize each item.

"Quiet, butthead," Jimmy whispered, abrasively. "Wait 'till my dad leaves," he said, a little on edge.

"Oh, right, my bad, *Jim*," Ryan snickered, covering his grin with his hand. Jimmy glared at him for a moment, and he glanced back to make sure his father hadn't heard anything.

"Relax, man," Ryan began, "he's just gonna think that we are camping out. He's not going to find out where," he told Jimmy, massaging his shoulders from the front.

Jimmy's father got out of their gray, 2018, S11 to speak with Ryan's mother, Ms. Trigee, who had come out on the porch to greet them. The boys jumped the fence and headed for the backdoor to Ryan's house.

"How's Jane?" she asked, smiling and folding her arms, while standing on the last step of their porch.

"She's good," replied Jimmy's father, walking through their yard to the porch.

"Please remind her that the school is giving free flu shots next week, and that she and Jimmy should get one."

"I will, thanks."

Ms. Trigee was Newford's school nurse and good friends with Jimmy's mother. Jimmy's father wanted to speak with her about the new school app that would allow the administration and the school nurse to send medical emergency alerts to parents.

"So, what do you think of the new app, Jean? It's one of the best out," said Jimmy's father, eagerly waiting for her reply.

"It's wonderful, John. Now, when a student becomes ill, all I have to do is text the parent using the app," Jean replied. "It's really easy to use."

"Yeah, we tech geeks use the term 'user-friendly' to describe that aspect," his father explained. His father took pride in his job, and he enjoyed helping teachers integrate technology into their classroom and into instruction.

While the parents spoke, the boys gathered in Ryan's room to organize the equipment and to hash out the details of their plan. The cave they had discovered was located about a mile down the road from Ryan's house. The boys knew that they would have to wade through a densely wooded area and run through a field to get to the hidden entrance. They also knew that their parents wouldn't allow them to go there alone, especially if the land was privately owned—which was a definite no-no, and would warrant a two-week grounding stint if they were caught.

Knock! Knock!

Ryan opened his door to see Jimmy's father.

"Hey, Mr. Rood," Ryan said, holding the door open for him.

"Hey, Ryan," he replied, standing near the threshold. "Okay, Son, I'll see you tomorrow about 10:00," he said, turning to Jimmy, and then glancing down at his watch. *He was always worried about the time, like he was an airline pilot afraid he was going to be late for liftoff.* Jimmy smiled to himself as he thought about his father's peculiar obsession with time.

"'kay, Dad," replied Jimmy, waving to his father as he shut Ryan's bedroom door.

Once Jimmy's father had left the house, the boys got back to work on their secret excursion.

"Okay, we have everything," Jimmy said, after taking note of all the supplies. "So, when are we doin' this?"

"Mom goes to bed around 10:00 P.M., so I figured we would sneak out a few minutes later," Ryan decided. "Once she is out, she won't hear a *damn* thing," he added with a chuckle.

"Okay, sounds good. Ten it is," retorted Jimmy with a confident grin.

As the boys waited for their adventure to commence, they decided to watch music videos and movies on Ryan's Z-box III. Ryan opened up a music app and began playing Jimmy's playlist of May Sting songs.

"Give 'em the Two Punch!" Jimmy sang. "Man I love May Sting. She can sing and she's *so* fine," Jimmy said with a sigh. "I wish I had a front-row seat at one of her concerts."

"Yeah, if you weren't so ugly, you might have a shot with her," Ryan replied, glancing at Jimmy with a large grin.

"Shut, up, idiot, no one cares what you think," retorted Jimmy, pretending to rebuke him.

"Just playin', man. I think you're cute; I would date you," Ryan said, reaching over to his left and running his fingers playfully through Jimmy's hair.

"Quit, you jackass! You know I don't roll that way!" Jimmy exclaimed, shrinking away, followed by simultaneous, boisterous laughter from both teenage boys.

Jimmy knew he wasn't the best looking fourteen-year old guy at Newford High, but he didn't feel that he was the worst looking one either. He had been on a couple of dates to the movies in the past few months, but those outings didn't lead to a relationship. He did, however, receive his first real kiss from one of the girls from Newford.

Her name was Lindsay Sweet, and they had gone to the movies together to watch *Star Tales V*. As her name implied, she was actually really sweet. Jimmy, however, thought this trait was a little annoying. He wanted a girl who was, in his father's words, a spitfire: one who wasn't afraid to say what she was thinking or to *think* for herself. He also felt his first kiss was just a little bit better than the one his grandmother gave him last Christmas.

As he watched May Sting singing and dancing, he imagined what it would be like to kiss her. He also imagined being on stage with her, singing "Two Punch," with his arm around her small waist, peering deep into her poignant, hazel eyes.

Ryan, observing that he was daydreaming about his life with her again, interrupted his fantasy.

"Now, don't get too excited...okay? Remember who and where you are," he laughed hard, leaning his head back on his Star Tale's bean bag.

"Oooh," Jimmy responded, giving Ryan a dirty look and holding up his right fist to eye level. Ryan closed his lips, trying to hold back his amusement. Jimmy put down his fist and glanced at Ryan with narrow eyes...and then grinned at him. He could never stay angry with Ryan, no matter how much or how hard he teased him.

Ryan, on the other hand, was an enigma of sorts. He didn't really try to date anyone, and most of the other teenagers thought he was unusually sensitive. He wouldn't admit to this, but his inclinations suggested otherwise. He never really spoke of admiring any of the girls at Newford High, nor did he really have a female celebrity crush, as most fourteen-year-old guys. If, however, he had wanted a girlfriend, then he wouldn't have much trouble finding one. It was well-known that many of girls his age thought he had pleasant features--with his short, curly black hair and light green eyes--and they also made comments about his courteous behavior toward them, not to mention his great sense of humor.

In fact, most teenagers at Newford High considered Ryan to be the school comedian, and he accepted this role with admiration, though it did, at times, give the teachers—and his mother—unbearable headaches. He would even dress the part, wearing the clothes that his favorite TV or movie characters wore.

That night, he was wearing a plain, green shirt with brown khakis and his black Star Tale's slippers. His entire room was decorated with Star Tale's paraphernalia. Jimmy knew that most of the students at Newford High laughed at him, not with him, but this didn't mean anything to Jimmy. He cared about Ryan, and he enjoyed being around him. They had been best friends since kindergarten, and nothing was going to change that.

When Ryan was around, Jimmy's mother and father treated him like part of the family. He guessed they did this because he had lost his father when he was three in an automobile accident, which they never attempted to discuss. It was just Ryan and his mother, so Jimmy ignored the special treatment by his parents--especially his father. He was like a brother to Jimmy, a really cool brother.

It was 10:05 P.M., and Ryan's mom was preparing for bed as usual. The boys were geared up and ready to move as soon as her bedroom lights were out.

"Are they out, yet?" Jimmy asked, impatiently.

"Yeah, they're out, now," Ryan answered. "Let's move."

They climbed out Ryan's bedroom window and headed down the dark, paved street toward the wooded area off the side of the road. When they arrived at the large, raised land mass, they paused for a minute to catch their breath. They had run about a mile down the road, and then another quarter mile through the wooded area to the massive mound.

"Okay, you ready?" Jimmy asked. "There's no going back now, man."

"Yeah, I think so," Ryan grinned, as Jimmy flashed the light in his face.

"Okay, here we go," Jimmy replied, resolutely.

The cave was pitch black, even during the day time, and drops of water could be heard just inside the entrance. They both could feel the small rocks crunching beneath their feet as they flashed their lights from top to bottom. They noticed there were different tunnels that branched off from the main one, but they decided to stay on course. They also observed the bat droppings at various places and the stalagmite, which they thought was cool.

"Oooh," Ryan muttered, "We're in the *bat* cave."

"Be quiet," Jimmy commanded. "I really don't wanna wake any *bat*s."

"Alright," Ryan consented. "But, I would sure like to collect a sample of their guano."

"Maybe, later. Let's keep movin'," Jimmy said, trying to keep Ryan focused.

Several minutes in, they chose a spot to set up camp for the night. They took out their light sticks, turned them on, and placed them in a large glass jar for light. They had planned to stay until dawn and then return home before Ryan's mom had emerged from her slumber. Once they had enough light, they pulled out their sleeping bags to sit for a few minutes. They also needed to regroup and to go over the plan one more time.

"Okay, so now we need to decide how much farther we are going to go tonight, right?" Jimmy asked, looking over at Ryan who had two glow sticks hanging out of his mouth. Jimmy held up a glow stick to his face, so Ryan could tell that he was serious. Ryan took the glow sticks out of his mouth.

"Yeah, I mean, there is no telling how far or deep this cave goes," he retorted. "Do we really want to go to the end tonight?" Ryan asked, apprehensively.

"I don't know about that, but I do wanna go farther," Jimmy replied. "Surely we are not the first ones to explore this cave, right?"

"I don't know, man, I didn't see any writing outside, no signs, nothing," Ryan answered. "Plus, the entrance was camouflaged by large blades of grass and long tree branches. Hell, we wouldn't have found it if you hadn't slipped and fell right in front of it," he chuckled to himself.

"Alright, well, let's drink these sodas, and then we will keep movin'," he said, popping the lid to one of the cans. "Let's get the rope out, too, and tie it off to that tree outside. I don't wanna fall down a hole and be stuck here, or get lost."

Jimmy and Ryan had been surfing the Internet for the past several weeks, making sure that they took every precaution before proceeding into the depths of the unknown cavern. Once they backtracked to tie off the rope, they trudged back to the dank place where they had set up camp. They unloaded what they could, and then continued on into the darkness of the cold, damp cave.

After several more minutes had passed, Jimmy saw a shiny object a few feet in front of him. He pointed his flashlight toward it.

"Dude, do you see that?" he asked, half-surprised and half-frightened. "Do you see that glow? What is that?"

"I don't know, man, but I think it's time to go," Ryan answered, nervously.

"No, wait, let's just see what it is, okay?" Jimmy stated, rhetorically.

As they both approached a wall and what they believed might be the end of their journey, they paused in front of the glowing object.

"What is it?" Ryan asked, astonished by what he saw.

"It looks like a ring, and it's a blue one," Jimmy replied, reaching down to pick it up. "I guess we weren't the first ones here, huh?"

Jimmy placed the ring in the palm of his left hand and moved it toward Ryan, so he could get a good look at it, too.

"I bet it's worth a fortune," Ryan stated, his eyes growing larger. "I bet it also belongs to someone," he said, taking out his phone to take a picture of the glittering object.

"Yeah, me," Jimmy said with a mischievous grin.

Jimmy placed the ring on his finger, and the large ring gripped it.

"No, way," he replied in amazement. "The ring just fitted me for size, bro."

"It...It just latched on to your finger!" Ryan replied, raising his voice.

"Quiet, man, were in a damn cave!" Jimmy retorted loudly.

"Put it back, and let's ball out!" Ryan exclaimed.

"*No*, I'm taking it with me," he said firmly.

"Okay, but let's go before the owner comes back," Ryan urged.

Once back at the campsite, they put out their glowing sticks, packed up their supplies and headed toward the entrance of the cave. Halfway to the opening, they heard a voice:

"Where do you think you are going with my ring?" The sinister voice asked.

The boys stopped in their tracks, frozen. Then, torches were lit, and three faces could be seen standing in the path between them and the way out of the cave. One of them, the middle one, was a white man, wearing gray army fatigues and had both his hands behind his back. He was adorned with military insignia, one of which had three silver stars. The other two, who were carrying the torches, were clothed in similar attire. The man in the middle, the one who was doing the speaking and obviously in charge, spoke again to the boys.

"Let me try this again," he said menacingly. "Where do you *think* you are going with my ring?"

This time the two of them could see that he was wearing glasses, had a thin, dark brown mustache, and his voice sounded foreign. His eyes appeared to be olive black, and they were steady, motionless, and fearsome. He freed one of his hands to show the boys another ring, but it was different from the one they had discovered. This one was ruby red.

"We ...We are sorry, Sir," Jimmy stammered, "We were just explorin' this cave of yours, and we accidently found it. Here, let me get it off my finger."

While Jimmy was trying to remove the ring, another voice could be heard from behind him.

"That won't be necessary, young man," the voice calmly stated.

Startled, the boys turned to see an older man with long, gray hair and a dark goatee, wearing all black and carrying a staff in one hand and a cane in the other, which provided him with ample light.

"Ori," the man with the foreign voice interjected. "So nice to see you again, my old friend. How have you been?" he continued casually. "I see your tailor is still the same, and you still have that illuminating cane and rotting staff," he chuckled sarcastically. "I'm afraid they won't be able to help you this time."

"Oh, I think they will do just fine, Gorlev," Ori said with a confident smile.

"Well, let us find out, then, shall we?" Gorlev retorted, threateningly.

Before the boys could do anything, the older man used his staff to whisk them aside into one of the adjacent walls. Gorlev quickly pointed his ring in the direction of Ori and flames appeared to shoot out of the sparkling ring. Ori twirled his staff to block the flames and to send the fire into a tunnel to his right, just over the heads of Jimmy and Ryan.

"Run behind me!" Ori shouted to the boys. "Head for the last tunnel on the right!" He shouted, using his staff to put out the torch lights. He quickly turned and followed the boys into the darkness.

Angry, Gorlev sent a beam of fire toward the feet of Ori. Ori, feeling the heat behind him, dove onto the cave floor, and the dust and smoke blew over him.

"I will smoke you out," Gorlev said, sending flame after flame through the cave. But, unable to bear the smoke of his own making, he backed out of the cave and waited. Moments later, scores of small bats stormed throughout the cave, making their exit through the opening.

"Ah!" Gorlev cried in dismay, trying to evade the swarm of bats. This gave Ori and the teenage boys a chance to escape.

The boys, running down the tunnel, paused for a moment as they came to a set of stone steps that led down to a nook in a wall, and light appeared to be coming from it. Ori, crawling as fast as he could to avoid being choked by the smoke, arrived at the steps, as the smoke billowed and enveloped the top and sides of the cave.

When Ori made it to the bottom of the stairs, he saw the boys standing by the nook in the wall. Ori looked at them and pointed to the nook.

Ori, coughing, "He's trying to smoke us out! Get into the nook; there's a way out from it!" he stated urgently, while trying to fight through a cloud of smoke.

The boys climbed into the nook and began crawling toward the light that was coming from the end of a passageway. Once they reached the end, they hopped down out of the opening and into a field. They took off running at full speed, not knowing where they were headed. They eventually came to a clearing with a few trees and an old cabin. They could see well enough through one of the cabin windows, and they saw a candle burning inside. They decided to hide there until the danger had passed.

As they entered, they saw a table where the candle was burning, a rocking chair, and a hearth with a pot hanging under it. They could smell the contents of it and were not impressed, but they were hungry. They assumed that this was the home of Ori, and they turned to see him coming into the clearing. When Ori arrived, he didn't say a word to them at first. He entered the cabin and sat down in his chair, breathing heavily, and he closed his eyes to rest for a few minutes.

The boys, who were too afraid to address the strange man, sat down and leaned against the wooden wall facing the fireplace. A few minutes passed, and then Ori opened his bright blue eyes and turned to gaze at the teenagers.

"Well, congratulations, boys, you have unlocked *Hades*. We Guardians thank you both," he said, agitated.

"We didn't mean to do anything," Jimmy said, honestly. "We were just exploring. We didn't know that the ring belonged to somebody. But, what do you *mean*?" he asked, sincerely.

Ori turned and made eye contact with Jimmy. He could see that Jimmy was being contrite. He also knew that Jimmy and Ryan were now involved in this situation, and he had to divulge its meaning, whether they were ready to hear it or not.

"Many Centuries ago...," he began softly, "mankind had lost faith in the gods, and the gods were losing their powers; they were dying. So, to protect the future of man and to help them to never forget the gods, Zeus ordered Hephaestus to create the Seven Rings of Man's Destiny. He ordered Athena to gather various powers from the gods, to supervise this endeavor, and to use her abilities to galvanize the rings. There are really six separate rings, with different powers, that can be combined to form, what we Guardians refer to as, the Zeus Ring. It is the seventh ring, the Golden Ring of Omnipotence...the ring that gives one person the authority of the gods on Earth. Zeus, realizing the ramifications of this decision, also ordered Athena to create the Guardians of the Rings, a secret organization of sorts, who were to protect the rings and the Ring Bearers from misuse or harm...from people like Gorlev, who undoubtedly, has decided to find all the rings and combine them to forge the Zeus Ring."

Ryan's eyes grew large and intense as he glanced at Jimmy's face and back to Ori's.

"I don't know about y'all, but I'm about to call the POH-lice," Ryan said, taking out his smartphone. "Dang! No service...What a shocker!" He continued, moving around the cabin to find a signal.

Jimmy ignored Ryan's theatrics for moment as he tried to grasp Ori's meaning.

"Oh, crap," Jimmy said, worried. "So, who has the other rings? And, if the Guardians are supposed to protect the rings, then how did Gorlev get one?" he asked, skeptically.

Ori, nostalgically, "In my lifetime, there was only one who was worthy of the Azure Ring of Water. *That* is the ring that I guard," he said, using his head to point to the ring on Jimmy's finger. "He became a physician, and he used the ring a few times to heal the sick, though I was never fortunate enough to witness such a marvel. He also used it to purify some water sources for people who didn't have clean water--but there are rules," he added, "Not every Ring Bearer chooses to follow them, and not every Ring Bearer is worthy of the rings."

"What happened to the physician?" Ryan inquired, giving up on a signal.

"He died about ten years ago, but he brought the ring back to me," Ori explained, sadly, and he looked down and away from Jimmy, as if he were hiding something. "I hid it in the cave; it has been there for over a decade, waiting for another prospective Ring Bearer to claim it."

Ori, continuing to explain, "Since Gorlev has one of the rings, then that means the Guardian of his ring either failed to train him properly, or Gorlev has chosen a different path. It rarely happens, but it is not uncommon. In Gorlev's case, it could also mean that his Guardian is dead," he said, sullenly. "A Guardian would never betray the oath."

"What are the *rings*?" Jimmy asked, after a few moments of silence.

"Well," Ori thought to himself, "There is the Ruby Ring of Fire, which you have seen courtesy of our friend, Gorlev. Then, there is the Emerald Ring of the Earth; there is the Amethyst Ring of Dominion; there is the Diamond Ring of Ice, and there is the Silver Ring of Prophecy...Oh, and then, there is your ring: The Azure Ring of Water," he said, completing the list of rings and pointing once again to the blue ring on Jimmy's finger.

"What do they *do*?" Jimmy asked, curiously.

"Well," he thought to himself again, "Some of the powers are more obvious. For instance, your ring controls water; the ring of fire, fire; and the ring of ice, ice. Others are not so conspicuous. Take the ring of dominion, for example: it can give its bearer the power to read and to control minds," he explained, mysteriously.

"So, *I* can control water?" Jimmy asked, skeptically, holding up his left hand to observe the ring carefully.

"If you wish, yes, after some training," replied Ori, candidly.

"What happens if I don't want the training?" he asked, timidly.

"You see this?" Ori asked, holding up his staff. "This azure object, same as the element and color of the ring on your finger, along with my cane, are both inventions of the gods. Hera empowered my staff through the blue element at the top, and Artemis produced the material for my staff, which is virtually indestructible--," he said, admiring it.

"Okay, suppose I believe you," Jimmy interrupted. "What *then*?"

"*Then*, you and your friend, if he chooses, will accompany me to find the next ring, which involves finding the next Guardian. You will also be trained, and your friend will learn to use my cane and my staff."

Ryan, overhearing Ori's explanation and reference to him, became interested.

"Where is the next ring?" Ryan questioned, taking a seat next to Jimmy against the wall of the cabin.

"The closest one is somewhere in South America. You see, the six rings were given to six Guardians on six of the seven continents. As a Guardian I can locate another Guardian and the particular ring that I protect. The closer I get, the easier it becomes for me to find another one of us. It's like Guardian radar," he said with a clever grin.

"Wait a minute...I can't go to South America. I have school Monday," Jimmy remembered. Reality and fantasy seemed to collide in his mind, and he could not decide what was real and what wasn't.

"Yeah, and what about our parents?" Ryan asked, incredulously, worried about having to leave his mother.

"Indeed! This would be a good time to have the ring of dominion," he stated, grinning again. "What you have failed to ask is how we are going to get there in the first place. He moved to the hearth and removed the pot. "There is a reason that I am here. This spot was chosen for the Guardian of the Azure Ring centuries ago, though it has changed quite a bit," he said, retrospectively.

"At the center of each chosen place is a hearth or some other means of teleporting--," he said casually.

"Wait! Did you just say, *teleporting*"? Jimmy interrupted once again.

"This just got real, *real* fast," Ryan said, looking at Jimmy, bewildered by this new information. "Okay, I'm ready to wake up now, *please!*" he said, looking up at the cabin ceiling and appearing to invoke a supernatural entity.

"Yes, though, former Guardians referred to these devices as the portals of the gods. See, you can leave through means of one of these channels; and, when you return, nothing has changed for those who are not participants. Time is different for the gods and those who use their portals. There are, of course, limitations on those who can use them: Guardians, their passengers, Ring Bearers, and gods. That's it," he said assuredly, as if any of his explanations made the teenage boys feel any better about their circumstances.

Just as Ori had finished speaking, they all heard footsteps outside the door.

"Quickly," Ori motioned to the hearth, "Get over here!"

Without thinking, the boys ran to the hearth, and Ori spoke the ancient words:

"In the name of the gods, give us Guardians passage!" he said with authority. As soon as Ori spoke the words, they were whisked away to another portal, where they would find the Guardian of another ring.

Chapter Two
The Hidden Place

Moments later Ori and the boys found themselves in a dimly lit room. They looked back and noticed that the fireplace was not like the rustic one at Ori's cabin, but was quaint and elegant. The boys scanned the room and observed that the light was coming from a lamp on a table in the corner of the yellow painted interior. They also saw a brown, leather recliner by another table, and a book lay on the surface.

"Oh, boy," Ori said to himself. "I don't think we are in South America. I may have allowed my concentration to switch to finding out what happened to Gorlev's Guardian. If, however, he is still alive...then he may be able to aid us," he explained.

"Where are we, then?" asked Jimmy.

"I believe that we are in Germany," Ori deduced, reading the title of the book on the table, which was in German. "The hometown of our friend, Gorlev."

"What! How did that happen? We've got to get outta here before that lunatic returns!" Ryan retorted, emphatically.

"Wait a minute," Ori stated calmly, holding his right hand in the air. "This is actually the one place where we may be safe for a while, the one place where he is not looking. He is after the rings, and I can sense a Guardian, which means that he or she is here," he paused to concentrate. "Though he or she may not be alive," he said, somberly.

"But, won't he come for us?" Jimmy questioned.

"Yes, once he realizes that we aren't in South America or another of the seven realms," Ori replied.

"What do you mean, *seven realms*?" Jimmy asked, overwhelmed, but still very intrigued by this new knowledge.

"Jimmy, there's a lot that I need to tell you. But, for now, let's see if our Guardian friend has anything good to eat," Ori answered, placing his hand over his growling stomach.

After wolfing down some beef soup, some bread, and drinking some German tea, the boys and Ori decided to find some blankets in the other rooms. Ori lit up the dark hallway and rooms with his cane. Ryan discovered a light switch and turned on the hallway light overhead.

"Found a light switch," Ryan said, smiling. "Not used to such luxury are you, Ori?"

"No, I guess not," he said with a grin, tapping his cane once in his hand to put out the illumination.

Ori opened the door to two rooms, and Jimmy went inside to flick on the lights. He saw blankets and pillows, so he gathered them up for the three of them. Ryan went into a third room and switched on the lights. He looked on the bed and gasped for air, before turning and looking at Ori in terror.

"What is it, son?" Ori asked, equally in terror. All Ryan could do was point. On the bed was a man who looked as if he had been torched to death, and the smell was putrid. Ori stepped in, and Ryan ran out. Jimmy caught him by the arm.

"What did you see, man?" he asked urgently.

"Let me go, Jimmy," Ryan pleaded, as tears began to roll down one cheek. Jimmy let him go, and Ryan quickly moved back into the first room. Ori had moved into the room already, and Jimmy moved in to join him. Neither of them spoke for a few minutes. Ori, cupping his chin with his left hand and placing his finger over his mouth, as if to think, was the first to speak.

"Here lies the Guardian of the Ruby Ring of Fire," he said in a matter of fact tone of voice. He turned to Jimmy and placed his hand on his left shoulder. "This is why we live: to protect and to die for the rings. He has done his creators a great service," Ori commented reverently, looking down on the floor beside the bed. The deceased Guardian's cane and staff were burnt down to a crisp. Ori surmised that Gorlev had murdered his Guardian in another place, and then decided to hide his body in the German dwelling. Nothing else had been burnt, and the body had been there for some time.

Jimmy remained silent, but he aided Ori in covering the dead Guardian. Ori kneeled beside the bed to honor him and to send him into the next life, reciting a prayer in Greek to Hades for repose and then to Athena for strength and protection.

Ori praying, "δώσει την ειρήνη, Hades," he paused. "παρέχουν προστασία, Athena," he said, as he ended his prayers.

36

As this was taking place, Jimmy moved back into the front room, sat down beside Ryan, who was sitting on a small, auburn sofa against the wall, and placed his arm around him. Ryan didn't look up right away, and Jimmy felt awful and responsible for getting him into this dangerous position.

"I'm sorry, man," Jimmy said, remorsefully. "I didn't know it would be this way. I just wanted to have some fun, you know? I'm always looking for adventure, something exciting, or something worthwhile that I can't get from my own life. Now that I have found it, I want to go back to my boring existence; I want to go home."

As Jimmy was speaking, Ori slipped into the room and sat down in the brown recliner by the table. They both turned around to see the pensive look on his face, and they waited to hear his reply, assuming he had heard everything that was said.

"I understand if you both would like to go home, and I am prepared to take you both back if that is what you both wish. It's just that I am getting older, and I don't know if I can fight this battle alone. Gorlev has likely gone to South America or to another realm to seek out another ring. The more rings he gathers, the harder it will be to stop him. When I look at you both, I see a Guardian apprentice and one chosen for this destiny," he said, while switching eye contact between the boys. "The choice, however, is *yours* to make, not mine, and there is no turning back once it is made," he said with a serious demeanor. "But, now, I think it is time to rest. It's been a very long and tumultuous day." And, with that he leaned back and drifted off to sleep.

The next morning, Jimmy and Ryan woke up and moved into the kitchen of the home and sat down at the table with Ori, who was drinking tea. The boys, after Ori had fallen asleep, stayed up and had come to a decision about whether to go home or stay and fight with Ori.

"We have made a decision," Jimmy said, looking to his left at Ryan and then back to Ori. "We are going to stay and let you train us to fight Gorlev."

"I see," Ori said, nodding his head in approval. "But, why did you two change your minds? It is clear to me that you both have the qualities that are required to be a Ring Bearer and, one day, a Guardian—but you will always have a *choice*. Gorlev was once like you, but then he made another *choice*. If you choose this life, then you must make good choices, and you must be ready to defend those choices. Do you understand?" he asked, making eye contact with both of them to check for comprehension.

"We believe that this fight is bigger than us, and we can't let Gorlev get all the rings and take control of the world. This is a fight that we can't back down from," Jimmy said, decisively. He glanced at Ryan as he ended his speech, and Ryan, inspired, nodded his head in agreement.

"Okay," nodding again, "Then let's begin your training. I know a secluded place where we can go. It's where I and many of the first Guardians went to train. It's a haven of sorts, and it's in Greece, the place of my birth, by a river and hidden forest. We should be safe there for a while. We may even run into another Guardian and Ring Bearer. Let's hope so," he said, grinning and getting up from his seat.

They each moved from the table to the fireplace to prepare to teleport. Ori said the words, and they were gone. Seconds later, they arrived in the hidden place of which Ori had spoken. There were four small huts in a clearing and a small fire near one of them. Ori motioned to the boys to be silent and to stay put while he went to investigate. He slowly pulled back the door to a hut. Just as he was about to enter the dark hut, a small figure leaped out and sprayed him with a barrage of ice, forcing him to fly away from the hut, over the fire, and on to his back in the dirt. A girl had jumped out and pointed her left arm in his direction, awaiting his response.

"Who are you?" she asked, menacingly. She saw the boys run to his side, but once they beheld what she had done to Ori, they slowed to a stop behind him. A man with a dark complexion moved out of the hut and took a place beside her with a cane strapped to his side and a staff in his right hand. Before Ori could get to his feet, the man noticed Ori's staff and cane by his side.

"You are a Guardian, too, then," the man said. Ori, still chilled from the ice pellets, made it to his feet with the boys by his side, as the girl watched them closely, her arm still stretched in their direction...as a drawn gun.

"I am Ori, Guardian of the Azure Ring of Water and the North American realm. This is Jimmy, owner of the Azure Ring and his friend, Ryan, a Guardian apprentice," he said, pointing to each of the boys. "We mean you no harm," he added, bowing to the dark man.

"I am Pazou, Guardian of the Diamond Ring of Ice and the Antarctica realm. This is Zoonee, owner of the Ice

Ring, as you can clearly see," he chuckled, pointing to the ring on her brown-tinted finger. "We have fled from a man who calls himself Gorlev and who accosted both of us in an attempt to steal the Ice Ring. We came here to hide and to train for battle," he explained in a deep voice.

Jimmy observed that he was a tall, slender man, like Ori, but not as old. He was more muscular, arrayed in all white, but he wore clothing that was similar to Ori's. He also observed that he had a scar down the side of his left cheek, which he imagined was made by a wild wolf or Polar Bear. *He looked like he could kill a Polar Bear*, he thought to himself. The man caught Jimmy staring at his scar, but simply smiled with his mouth closed. Jimmy looked away immediately.

"We are also here to hide and to train, and we, too, are fleeing from Gorlev until the boys are ready for him," Ori said, sighing in relief. Pazou motioned to Zoonee to relax herself and they both approached to greet Ori and the teenage boys.

Later that night, as they all sat around the small fire eating what the forest and a river provided, Ori asked Zoonee about her origins. Zoonee, glancing over at Pazou for permission, looked at the boys and back to Ori before speaking.

"I'm from Antarctica, one of the last few Chilean settlements from the realm. One day my family and I were out fishing, and we fell through the ice. I managed to grab hold of a block of ice, and I rode the block of ice. Pazou saw me and rescued me, and we have been family ever since. My parents drowned...I was ten, but my grandmother and cousins are still alive. One day, I plan to see them again," she said sadly, looking down into the fire. "But, first, I will fulfill my obligations to Pazou and stop this man who controls fire," she said, gazing at Jimmy and his ring.

"Do you know how to use it yet?" she asked, doubtfully.

"No, I haven't been trained," he said looking downward at the ground, avoiding eye contact. He observed that she was wearing a hand-made, gray-colored, sleeveless shirt with hand-made, gray-colored pants, and she was also wearing grey gloves with the fingers cut out of them. She had short, black hair, jet-black eyes, and a brown complexion. He found himself attracted to her appearance, her charisma, and her loyalty to the dark-skinned Guardian. He wanted to look her in the eyes, but he was too shy.

"Well, you better get a move on it," she suggested. Jimmy could only nod his head in response. Pazou smiled in her direction, and then he looked at Ori. Ori observed that he was clothed in all white, even his sandals were white.

"So, what do you know about Gorlev?" Pazou inquired.

"I met Gorlev several years ago. He murdered...," Ori paused, and then he began again. "Gorlev is the owner of the Ruby Ring of Fire, but he slayed the Guardian of the ring. I believe the Guardian saw something evil in Gorlev, and he tried to take back the ring. I believe he is trying to collect them all in an effort to forge the Zeus Ring," he said, with a look of dread. Pazou, grasping the weight of what Ori had relayed to him, reciprocated with one of his own.

"So, the only answer is to stop him from gathering the other rings, which means he must die," he replied, candidly. Ori looked up at him and nodded in agreement. Then, he turned to the boys.

"Your training starts at dawn, boys. Get some rest," he said, and then he made his way to one of the four huts. The boys said good night to the two new friends and made their way to a hut as well.

The next morning, the boys woke up to Ori standing over them:

"Okay, let's go, boys," he said, authoritatively. He told Ryan to stay behind, while he led Jimmy up to a cliff overlooking a green river. "This is where it begins," he said, facing the green river. "I can remember bringing the physician here and watching him create and control the green water," he said, with a reminiscent smile. "Hold out your arm, and point the ring at the river." Jimmy did as he was told. "Now, relax, and let the ring fill you with its power."

"I can...feel it," Jimmy said, amazed.

"Yes, when it fills you completely, then command it to move the water in the river," he instructed. Jimmy could feel its strength coursing through his body. His eyes began to glow bright blue and an azure aura surrounded his body, glowing like the ring, and then he spoke:

"Move!" he commanded. Suddenly, the river waters began to rise up. Ori, seeing this spectacle, turned to him.

"Control it! Move it in any direction," he instructed. "Use its power, Jimmy! You are its owner, now." Hearing this, his confidence grew, and he lifted the water up over the cliff before them. Seeing this, Ori nervously retreated a few feet out of the way of the umbrella-like display above them. Jimmy then sent the wave of water flying into the trees across the river. The wave uprooted a few small trees and branches broke easily from the impact. Jimmy lowered his arm, as the waters receded. His eyes quit glowing and the aura disappeared, and he stood on the cliff, trying to absorb the event. Ori came to his side and placed his left hand on his right shoulder.

"Powerful, isn't it?" he asked, rhetorically, with a grin. Jimmy turned and smiled at Ori.

"Yeah, powerful," he agreed. "What else can it *do*?"

"Anything you can imagine, but you have to discover it, and that takes time, practice, and patience. When you're ready, you will be able to create water out of *nothing*, and even manipulate it," he stated, making eye contact with Jimmy. "After some time, the ring will obey your

45

thoughts, not just your voice. Stay here and practice while I attend to Ryan's training. I will send him for you at dusk." Ori turned and left Jimmy on the cliff to practice.

As Jimmy continued to practice, Zoonee crept up behind him. She had been watching him try to communicate with the ring in order to create water in his hand. She could see that he was struggling and offered to assist him.

"Uh, you're doing it wrong," she said correctively. She walked over to him and sat down, just a few feet from the edge of the cliff.

"Oh, hi!" he replied, startled and a little embarrassed.

"Watch me, okay," she said, as she sat down at the edge of the cliff with her legs crossed. "You have to let the ring's essence get used to you first. Then, you can create it." He watched as she seemed to be meditating, and then her eyes began to glow bright white and a white aura surrounded her petite figure. Shards of ice appeared to shoot up out of her hands, but they didn't go anywhere. Then she stood up and projected a large layer of ice across the green river.

After she had finished, Jimmy realized that she had made an ice bridge from the cliff to the other side of the river. He was fascinated by her confidence and the casual exhibition of her skills. He was also grateful for her advice and demonstration.

"Let's slide down it," she said with a smile, displaying her ivory teeth. Not wanting to disappoint her, he jumped on the ice bridge and slid down it to the other side of the river.

When they reached the other side, they smiled at each other.

"How do we get back?" Jimmy asked. "I'll never make it."

"With me, silly," she said with an arrogant, yet playful smile. "I could freeze the entire river if I wanted to." She paused to take in her surroundings.

Changing her tone: "It is a beautiful jade river, isn't it?" Jimmy, having already seen the river, now stared at her face.

"Yes, it is beautiful," he admired. Zoonee turned to him and could see that he was not looking at the river—but at her profile. Pretending that she hadn't noticed him watching her, she proceeded to instruct him.

"You see, you have to get to know the ring; communicate with it. It has to be a part of you. Once this happens, you won't have to order it to do anything. It will just know," she stated wisely.

The two of them visited until it was about dusk, and then they decided that they had better head back to the huts. Zoonee motioned to him and told him to take her hand. Then, without much warning, she began to skate up the ice bridge back to the cliff.

"Don't let go," Jimmy said, looking down from the ice bridge into the green river. Zoonee turned and smiled.

"Don't worry, Jimmy," she reassured him, "You will be safe with me. Just follow my lead and let your feet glide up the ice with mine."

When they reached the top, they both hopped off the bridge simultaneously. They laughed and headed down the path to the campsite. On the way there, Jimmy wondered about the bridge and what would happen to it.

"What about the bridge?" he asked, curious.

"The bridge will melt by morning. It's just ice, you know. Of course, I could take it down, if I wanted to," she told him confidently.

"How long did it take you to master your ring's power?"

"A couple of years," she admitted. "I started when I was twelve, but I'm not sure that I have mastered it. Pazou would say that I still have more to learn." She looked over at Jimmy, making eye contact with him. "You don't have to master it to use it, Jimmy."

Jimmy thought about this information for several minutes. He had another question for her.

"Okay, so, I get where most of the powers come from, you know, like fire, Prometheus; water, Poseidon; and Ori told us about his. But, where does the power of ice come from?" he asked, somewhat puzzled, glancing over to his right at Zoonee.

Zoonee, beamed with delight at his query. "It comes from the goddess Chion. She is the goddess of ice and snow. You might wanna brush up on your mythology, Jimmy," she suggested, grinning at him.

"Yeah," he said, a little abashed, as he pushed his hair away from his face.

When they had reached the campsite, Ryan came running up to greet them. He was carrying Ori's staff and wanted to show Jimmy what he had learned to do with it. Without saying a word, he twirled the staff around his body, creating a vortex of wind around himself. Jimmy and Zoonee paused, mouths agape, to witness his new skills in action. After twirling it for a few minutes, he released the wind toward a thicket to the east of them. The wind blew a path through it, uprooting much of the shrubbery in its way, and knocking over a few small bushes.

"Man, that move was awesome!" Jimmy exclaimed. "You should see what Zoonee can do. It is cold, really *cold*," he smiled at his play on words.

"Thanks, dude," he said delighted by the adulation. "Ori taught me that in just a few hours. What did you two *do*, today?" Sensing his double meaning, Jimmy spoke quickly.

"I made a big wave and moved it above me and Ori. Zoonee, made an ice bridge out of thin air, and we slid down it," he said, excited.

"How'd you guys get back up it?" he teased again. He smiled mischievously at Jimmy and glanced at Zoonee in the same manner. Zoonee, now sensing his humorous purpose, glowered back at him. He observed her disposition and thought it best to stop teasing them. He had seen what she had done to Ori the first day, so he quickly changed the subject and tone of the conversation.

"Ori wants to talk to you in his hut," he said, somewhat timidly.

"Okay, thanks, dude," Jimmy replied, heading to Ori's hut. He went inside and Ori, drinking a cup of tea made from bamboo, motioned to him to sit down. He finished what was in his cup, and then he looked up at him and smiled.

"So, how did it go, today?" he asked, interested.

"Great! Zoonee told me to try to talk with the ring, like real a person. She said that the ring needed to get to know me. Then I won't have to say anything at all. Is she right?" he asked.

"Yes, she is right, but there is more you should know about the ring," he answered. "The ring does far more than what you have seen, and it represents more than you know. Some Guardians believe that your ring is the most powerful of the rings," he added, cryptically.

"But, I thought the Zeus Ring was?" Jimmy questioned.

"The Zeus Ring is the most powerful ring because it is a combination of all the powers belonging to the rings. In and of itself, the Zeus Ring is simply a mythical object. We have never seen it. But, like the other rings, we believe that it could become a reality. Your new friend, Zoonee, can only see what it does, but she still doesn't comprehend its real power, though I imagine that she's not far from it."

"Ori, I'm a teenager. You need to break this stuff down for me," he retorted, overwhelmed by Ori's wisdom.

"Okay, take Zoonee, for instance. She is the owner of the Diamond Ring of Ice. She can create and control the ice component. But, she must learn that ice is not an offensive weapon. It preserves, shields, and heals. She must learn this for herself," he explained. "When she does, then she will be able to unlock its real powers."

"So, I guess I need to find these powers for myself," Jimmy inferred.

"Yes, I'm afraid so," he empathized. "But it won't take too long—just be patient and try to stay focused. At about that time, Pazou broke in and told them it was time eat; he had been hunting all day for food. They both stood up and went outside by the fire. Zoonee and Ryan were already there, sitting across from each other. Ryan, who was still wary of Zoonee, attempted to communicate with her.

"You like Jimmy, huh?" he continued teasing.

"Yes, I do," she admitted. "He is a good friend: honest, brave, and loyal. He would have to be, to be here."

"Do you think he's hansom?" he asked, grinning cantankerously. Zoonee was writing something in the dirt, but she was also listening intently. She raised her head and glared at him.

"Do you *like* the use of your fingers?" she scowled. Ryan's vivacious grin faded as he lowered his head. Pazou, overhearing the banter, stepped in to ease the tension.

"Easy, Zoonee, he's only joking. He is a friend, too," he said, in an effort to calm her. Zoonee acknowledged him and moved over to allow Pazou to sit down, continuing to draw in the dirt. Ori sat down beside Pazou, and Jimmy sat straight across from Zoonee beside Ryan. Zoonee quit her drawing, for moment, to glance into Jimmy's eyes which were always on her. She observed this and pointed her head back down, beaming about something that was hidden from everyone else.

After eating the boys and Zoonee decided to practice using their abilities on a boulder to one side of the clearing. Zoonee went first, showing the boys that she could freeze the large rock. Ryan used Ori's staff to relocate the boulder several feet to the left, landing with a crashing sound. Then it was Jimmy's turn. There was no water present, so Jimmy knew he had to apply what Ori and Zoonee had instructed him to do earlier. He knew he had to focus and communicate with his ring.

Ori and Pazou walked up behind them to watch the display of skills. Jimmy took a deep breath and then became silent for a few minutes. Ryan and Zoonee watched his face, waiting for him to do something. Jimmy could feel the ring's energy building inside of him. His eyes began glowing, along with his body, and he could feel the aura around him, producing a bright, azure- colored light. He remembered what Ori had told him, and he allowed the power of the ring to branch out through his mind. Finally, he shared his thoughts with the essence of the ring, held out his arm toward the boulder, and water appeared underneath it, pushing it upward until it was at eye level. With everyone watching in awe, Jimmy moved the boulder back to its original spot.

After it was over, Jimmy was exhausted, but ecstatic about what he had accomplished. Zoonee and Ryan came over to congratulate him, while Ori and Pazou looked on with approval. Zoonee hugged Jimmy, which pleasantly surprised him, and then she walked toward Pazou, glancing back to smile at Jimmy. Ryan, taking it all in, tried not to laugh, but he knew something special was developing between the two Ring Bearers.

"Way to go, man! You did it, Jimmy!" Ryan said enthusiastically, patting him on the back. "Zoonee liked it, too," he teased. Jimmy smiled and then punched him in the arm. Ryan acted as if he were going to hit Jimmy with his staff, but then he paused and grinned back at him. Ori and Pazou came over to praise Jimmy for his achievement.

"You are on your way, kid," Ori said, putting his hand on top of his head. "And, so are you, young student." He grabbed Ryan by both arms as he acknowledged him. "Come, time to rest. There is more to come," he said, placing his arms around them. Then he led them back to the huts to sleep for the night.

The next day, Jimmy and Ryan woke up, got ready, and were out of the hut before sun- rise. They went to Zoonee and Pazou's hut to wake her, but Zoonee was already awake and ready. Ori and Pazou remained asleep. They headed to the cliff to begin their training for the day. Once they arrived, they decided to take turns displaying and practicing their powers. Zoonee produced a barrage of large ice balls and aimed for a large tree across the green river. They hit the tree with such force that the tree finally fell backwards into another tree.

As Jimmy was preparing to create water, an Ochia Snake slithered within a couple of feet of him and began to raise its head, warning them in advance that they needed to leave the cliff. Jimmy, startled by the large snake, turned quickly toward it. The snake struck out at him, but Zoonee froze it in mid strike, causing it to fall short of Jimmy's shin. Ryan, using his staff and the force of wind, flung the snake off the cliff and into the river.

"Thanks," he said, gratefully. "But, we need to save the snake," he pointed at the snake floating, frozen, down the river.

"Why?" Ryan asked, flabbergasted. "It tried to bite you, dude."

"Because it was only defending its territory," Jimmy replied. Zoonee, grasping his message, used her powers to break the ice, and then Jimmy used the water to slide the snake up on the shore on the other side of the river. They all looked back and forth at each other for a few moments, and realized the responsibilities they each shared. They weren't just training to defeat their enemy anymore; they were training to be the stewards and protectors of the Earth. The magnitude of this revelation caused several minutes of silence and reflection, as they each sat down in their respective positions. While they were sitting, Zoonee looked at Ryan, and Ryan looked back at her, both realizing that Jimmy had become their leader.

Zoonee spoke first: "I'm with you Jimmy, no matter what happens," she said with conviction, maintaining eye contact with Jimmy.

Then, Ryan spoke up: "Me, too, man, 'till the end," he said with resolve. Jimmy knew from that moment that they had become a team, and he also knew that they had made him their leader. He glanced at each of them in turn and nodded his head in confirmation of his new role.

Chapter Three
The First Move

After they had finished training for the day, they all headed back to the campsite. When Jimmy got back, he felt that he needed to consult with Ori about the recent revelation he and his friends had had while practicing. He asked to come into Ori's hut, and Ori permitted him. Once inside, he observed that Ori and Pazou were developing a plan of action to stop Gorlev.

"Hey, Ori, can we talk, please?" he asked, respectfully. At this, Pazou smiled, got up, and patted Jimmy on the shoulder on his way out of the hut.

"How can I help, Jimmy?" he asked, turning his attention to him.

"I don't really know how to explain it, but I think Ryan and Zoonee now see me as their leader. I'm grateful, but I'm worried that--," he said, honestly.

"You are worried that you will fail them, right?" he interpreted, predicting the rest of Jimmy's statement.

"Yes," he answered. "I'm not sure that I'm ready to be anyone's leader. I'm not even sure that I can lead myself."

"That is a sign of a great leader, Jimmy, when you begin to care more about your followers, than yourself," he stated, proudly. "You are also beginning to accept your destiny, another true sign of a great leader."

"So, there's nothing wrong with me?" he asked, self-consciously, raising his left eyebrow.

"No, there are many things that are *right* about you, Jimmy," he assured him. "You have many outstanding qualities that would make you a successful leader."

"Okay, that makes me feel a little better," he said, relieved. "So, what were you and Pazou talking about?" he asked, changing the subject.

"We believe that Gorlev will eventually come to this place. We even think that he wants us to be here, so he can gather us all in one spot," he said, concerned. He pulled on his goatee for a few minutes before speaking again. "We don't have much time."

"Speaking of time, I thought it was different for Guardians and Ring Bearers," Jimmy replied, puzzled.

"True. Time for us is sidereal, as it was for the gods, which allows us to manipulate it by means of the teleport, a creation of the gods. Unfortunately, Gorlev knows how to do this as well," he said, distraughtly. "He may not be worthy of the rings, but he is still a Ring Bearer."

"What do you mean, 'as it was for the gods,'" he asked, intrigued.

"Well, the gods rely on the constellations and the planets for their time, just as we do. But, they use more than we do. The older Guardians used to say that time is relative to each planet, that the gods connected each teleport to a specific planet. Which, of course, is unknown to us. They also used to say that the planets are the tombs of the gods. But, who knows, right?" he grinned, feeling better that Jimmy had distracted him. "Anything else?"

"No, that's plenty," he said, feeling a bit overloaded with knowledge. Ori chuckled and asked him to send Pazou back into the hut.

Jimmy went over to sit down with Zoonee and Ryan around the campfire. He wanted to sit by Zoonee, but he didn't have the courage.

"What's up, man?" Ryan asked. "Is everything okay?" He looked to his left to view Jimmy's facial expressions. Jimmy, taking to heart what Ori had told him, didn't want to tell them the truth. He didn't want to dishearten them after all the success that they had made. He decided to give them the general ideas, but skew the details a bit.

"He basically said that he and Pazou are preparing for Gorlev, and we should simply continue with training until they let us know when it's time to put their plan into action," he said, hoping they would buy it and not ask too many questions. They both looked at him, but he wouldn't make eye contact with either one of them. They knew he was hiding something from them, but they didn't ask.

Ryan yawned and then got up: "Well, good night, you guys. We've got another day of training tomorrow," he said. He waved to them both and headed for the hut. For a few minutes, Jimmy and Zoonee had to face an awkward silence. Then Zoonee, checking to make sure that Ryan was in the hut, moved over to sit by Jimmy.

"So, what's your family like," she asked, curiously.

"Oh, uh, my dad is a tech at Newford High School. He spends most of his day running cables through walls, replacing hardware, and updating software for computers. Oh, and if the server goes down, he has to fix it. Do you know what a computer is?" he asked, ignorantly.

"Yes, silly," she smirked, "I *did* go to school in Antarctica, though it was very small. It was in a research facility. They had computers and *everything*," she said, teasing him. "We lived on a research base for families of fishermen, until the accident," she added, morosely. "Pazou found me, saved me, and now we are here."

"My bad," he apologized, blushing. "I didn't know. All I know about Antarctica are Eskimos and whales," he admitted, raising both of his hands halfway in the air.

"You may be thinking of Alaska, but that's okay. Go on," she demanded. "What about your mother?" What does she do?"

"My mom is a secretary for the junior high school in Newford," he replied, glancing back and forth at her face. She spends most of her day at a desk, taking messages and making people wait...You know," he said, beaming at her. "I would show you some pictures, but my phone's battery is dead, and I didn't bring my charger. What did your parents do?"

"My mother was a *mother*. She took care of me, but she would help my dad fish sometimes. My father was a fisherman; his father was a fisherman. My father caught fish for a company onboard a ship. They usually caught krill. It's a very dangerous job," she said, sullenly.

"Are you kiddin'?" he said, excited, and trying to cheer her up. "I bet they saw killer whales all the time. How cool is that? Your dad was *Boss*!"

Zoonee didn't respond right away. She just stared at him and his grin. She wasn't sure what to think of him, but she knew how he made her feel.

Jimmy, unable to bear the awkward silence and unsure how to read hers, started over again.

"I think it takes a lot of courage to do what your parents did to survive. I don't know if I could do it," he said, humbly.

Zoonee turned and smiled at him, appreciating his kind answer. She reached down and took his hand. Jimmy, surprised, looked up into her deep, dark eyes and grinned at her. Zoonee edged a little closer to him and placed his hand on her leg, peering down into the campfire.

A few minutes later...

"I think you *could*, Jimmy," she stated, confidently.

Just then, Pazou and Ori came out of the hut, and Zoonee dropped Jimmy's hand and moved back across the campfire to sit down. Ori and Pazou looked at both of them and grinned, inferring what was taking place between the two of them. They glanced at each other and then back at them. Jimmy's face was frozen red, as he stared in terror at the two Guardians.

"It's time for rest," Pazou instructed, looking at Zoonee. "Good night, Mr. Jimmy," Pazou said, grinning.

"Good night, Jimmy," Zoonee said as she waved timidly. Ori sat down beside Jimmy. For a few moments, they didn't speak.

"She's a pretty girl, Jimmy," he said, intuitively. "She's also a strong soul," he added.

"Yes, she is --a strong soul," he replied, not wanting to admit that he found her attractive.

"I may not be the right person to tell you this, and you may not be quite ready to hear it, but being alone is a difficult choice. When I had learned that my bloodline had been chosen for this destiny, I made the decision to be alone. There is nothing that I regret more than making it," he said, sincerely.

"Was there ever a girl in your life?" Jimmy asked, interested.

"Yes, here in Greece," he replied, reflectively. "Her name was Leedi, and she was cheerful, compassionate, and strong. She had been a good friend to me for a long time. But, as we grew older, our feelings for each other grew as well. That was about the time that I learned that my fate had been predetermined by the gods. I was fourteen: your age. Before I knew it, I was here training with my father, as his apprentice."

"But, was she pretty?" Jimmy asked. Ori, grinning to himself and understanding Jimmy's perspective, placed his hand on his left shoulder.

"Incredibly," he replied, getting up and heading for his hut. Jimmy waited, trying to process the wisdom Ori had shared with him this time. He knew that he liked Zoonee, and he felt like it could be more. But, he was afraid for her. He didn't want her to get hurt, so he knew he, like Ori, would have to make a tough choice.

After contemplating his feelings, he stood up and went toward his hut for the night.

The next morning, the boys woke up and could hear faint whispers from just beyond their hut. They each roused themselves and headed outside to find out what was going on and who was speaking. They saw Ori and Zoonee waving farewell to Pazou, and they approached the two of them. When Pazou reached the edge of the clearing, he said the ancient words, and then he teleported out of their sight.

Zoonee, visibly angry with Ori, was arguing with him in the center of the clearing.

"Who do you think you are?" she asked, vehemently. "He is my Guardian! You may have sent him to his death!"

"Someone had to go to South America to find another Ring Bearer and to see what we could find out about Gorlev's recent activities. Pazou decided that it would be better for him to go and for us to stay to continue with training," he calmly replied.

"I should be with him," she glowered at Ori. "You are too reckless with your decisions." She turned before Ori could reply and stomped off to her hut without acknowledging either of the boys. Ori, grieved by Zoonee's derision, gave the boys a half-hearted smile and then proceeded back to his hut. Not really knowing how to take what they had just witnessed, the two of them went to Zoonee's hut to see about her. Jimmy carefully peaked inside her hut.

"You, okay?" he asked softly, concerned. Zoonee was facing the other way and didn't reply right away. Jimmy slowly slipped in behind her and placed his hands on her shoulders. Zoonee, weeping, placed her right hand on one of his.

"Pazou has been like a father to me since I was ten," she said, wiping a tear off the side of her right cheek, but keeping her right hand on Jimmy's. Jimmy, apprehensive, took a chance and placed his arms around her.

"My father is so busy with his work that he doesn't spend much time with me," he said, honestly. "Ori spends time with me, and he listens. I trust him, and I think you can, too." Jimmy gave her tiny waist a squeeze as he spoke.

"I believe you, Jimmy, but I'm not sure about Ori. He will have to prove himself to me, first. He isn't off to a good start," she said, frankly.

"Fair enough," he replied. "So, why don't we try to hunt down some breakfast?" he asked, trying to lighten the mood.

"Ugh, boys," she said. "All they think about is food." They both laughed and headed outside to hunt. Ryan was sitting by the campfire with Ori's staff in hand. He looked up as they came closer to him.

"So, how's it going, lovers," he grinned. "Don't think I don't see it. Everyone in this clearing knows." Zoonee and Jimmy looked at each other and laughed.

"Mind your own business," Zoonee warned, half-smiling.

"Yes, Ma'am, he replied," bowing to her. Zoonee glared at Ryan and then looked back at Jimmy.

"Can I freeze him? Can I *please* freeze him? Just once?" she asked, pretending to be irritated at Ryan. Jimmy grinned, reaching down for her hand, and led her off into the woods.

Ryan, calling after them: "Hey, bring me back a cheeseburger, will ya?" he asked, jokingly.

After they were out of sight, Ryan headed for Ori's hut. He poked his head in to see if he could chat with him. Ori, looking somewhat perturbed, motioned to him, giving him permission to come into the hut.

"How are you, Ryan?" he inquired. Ryan, looking as if he wanted to get something off his chest, spoke plainly.

"Does Gorlev know that we are here?" he questioned. Ori sensed that he couldn't keep the truth from him any longer. He spoke just as plainly to him.

"Most likely, yes, but this is why Pazou and I felt that we needed to make a first move. He has chosen to go to South America, hoping that he will find the Guardian of the Emerald Ring of the Earth before Gorlev gets to him. Hopefully, this Guardian has found and trained his Ring Bearer. If so, then they can help us defeat him." Ryan, with a pensive look, wanted to know more.

"Were we chosen for this? Like you?" he asked, reflectively.

"Yes, but not like I was chosen. My future was predetermined centuries ago. But, you, Jimmy, and Zoonee had a choice. You all *chose* to be *chosen*," he said, cryptically. "Think of it as a *team* that you *chose* to join. Each member of your team has a role to play in the mission or goals of the team. Each member is also responsible for his or her teammates. Does this make sense?" he asked him to see if he understood his analogy.

"Yeah, it does. But what about me? Why did you choose me to be a Guardian? Why not Jimmy?" he queried.

"Jimmy *chose* the ring, and with it, all of its responsibility and power. There can only be one Ring Bearer and only one Guardian apprentice. I chose you, Ryan, because you chose to follow your friend. I chose you because of your loyalty, dedication, and courage," he said with an approving smile.

Ryan, thinking about his father, decided to confide in Ori:

"My father died when I was little. Ever since then, it has just been me and my mom. Jimmy was my first friend that I made when we moved to Newford. He and I have been buddies for a long time, and that is why I chose to do this...because of him. He has helped me through some tough times."

Ori nodding, "I understand, and I'm sorry to hear about your father. I would never try to take his place; but, if you ever need to talk, I'm here for you, too." Ryan looked up and smiled at Ori, and Ori reciprocated with one of his own. Deep down, Ryan knew he needed a father figure, and Ori had just applied for the job. This made Ryan exceedingly happy and more comfortable with Ori. Ryan felt that he was now mentally prepared and committed to being a Guardian apprentice.

"I think it is time for us to start today's training," Ori said. Ryan stood up in agreement, and they both headed outside.

Chapter Four
The New Guy

Now that Jimmy had developed his skills with the Azure Ring, fishing was relatively easy. He was able to wade into the jade river and snare trout in his water traps. Since he had grown up in a fishing town, he knew how to fillet and to fry the fish. Zoonee, having come from a family who made their living fishing, knew how to do this as well. They believed that they were the perfect fishing team.

"I got another one," Jimmy said, excited. "This one is a rainbow trout." He placed the fish in an ice bowl that Zoonee had created. "That ought to be enough, right?"

"Four, five, six,--" she counted. "Yes, that should do it."

"Let's go get some more figs from that one tree Ori showed us last time," he suggested. "Then we'll be ready to cook this grub." Zoonee chuckled at Jimmy's comment as she helped him fillet the fish.

As they walked back to camp, Zoonee reached out to hold Jimmy's hand. Jimmy accepted her hand, glanced into her eyes, and they headed back hand-in-hand. Jimmy was about five or six inches taller than Zoonee, so he was able to sneak a peek at her without being detected. She made him feel important, and he made her feel special.

As soon as they made it back to the clearing, they dropped hands, not because they were ashamed of how they felt toward one another, but because they didn't want to be a distraction or to be endlessly teased by Ryan. They saw Ori, Ryan, and two others at the campsite. They could somehow sense that something was amiss, and they looked at each other, their eyebrows shaped in the form of a V, wondering what the matter was. The closer they came to the others, the easier it was for them to see that someone was lying on the ground in front of them. Zoonee, seeing that it was Pazou, gasped and ran to his side. Jimmy quickly followed behind her.

"Pazou!" she shouted. She kneeled down beside him and grabbed his right arm, looking down into his face. Ori was supporting his frame, so only the lower half of his body was touching the cold ground. "What happened?"

"He was badly burned by Gorlev, trying to rescue the young man behind you. We need to move him to the hut to make him more comfortable," he said, urgently. They all helped Ori move Pazou inside his hut. They all followed.

Zoonee, irate, "Look what you did to him, you foolish man! I told you that you should have allowed me to go with him. Who is this? What is he doing here?" She glared at the young man with dark hair, coal-colored eyes, and a tanned complexion. She was too distracted to notice what everyone else did: That he was wearing a bright, emerald ring.

"Zoonee, it is not his fault!" Pazou said in an authoritative tone. Zoonee wasn't comforted by his assertion, but she was forever obedient and loyal to Pazou. She kneeled down beside him, with a somber disposition, knowing she had displeased him.

"I'm sorry, Pazou," she said sullenly. Pazou reached out for her and patted her on one of her hands.

"You are a good child, and I will forever be grateful for having found you," he said in a parental voice. "But, now, you must be strong for me, okay?"

"Yes, Pazou, I will," she replied, tears falling from her eyes.

Ori asked them to bring Pazou some water and to move outside to allow him to rest. They all moved out of the hut and gathered around the fire. No one made a sound, and no one asked about the young man sitting by himself on the other side of the campfire. Several minutes later, Ori emerged from the hut and motioned for them to gather around him.

Ori sighing, "Okay, this is what we know. Sitting across from you is Parelo from South America. He is the Emerald Ring Bearer of the Earth. His Guardian, Sazzo, was killed by Gorlev and his men. Pazou managed to dispatch one of Gorlev's men, but Gorlev was able to inflict serious injury upon him before he escaped with Parelo. Ori, looking at the mysterious young man, "I was hoping you could shed some light on what actually happened. The details might be of some use to us when we battle Gorlev and his men."

Parelo, looking around at all of them, "Me and Sazzo were running and hiding from Gorlev when Pazou found us in a small Brazilian town. He had four men with him with guns. When they found us, they threatened to shoot us or torch us if we didn't hand over the Emerald Ring. Pazou used his staff to disarm the men, but Gorlev was able to create fire and throw flaming balls at him and Sazzo. I used the ring to summon a puma to chase the men, but the men had small guns and shot and killed the puma," he reflected, sadly. "Sazzo became angry at this, and used his staff to throw one of the men into a large tree, killing him. But, Gorlev was too much. He created a fire lasso and wrapped up Sazzo, choking him to death with the smoke. I used the ring to create a pit beneath him, trapping him long enough for us to make our escape to this place. I...I didn't know Pazou had been injured until we arrived. He must have been hit by one of the flaming balls of fire Gorlev had unleashed upon us. I am truly sorry. He saved my life."

Zoonee, with tears coming down her cheeks, "What will happen to Pazou? Will he die?" Ori moved over to her and placed his left arm around her shoulder.

Ori, thinking aloud, "Maybe not. He is not dead, and he can be healed," he said, looking around at Parelo. How far did you get into your training, son? I have heard that the Earth ring has healing powers, powers from Artemis herself."

"I can try, but don't know for certain. Sazzo trained me well enough, but I've never used the ring's power to heal," he regretted.

"We would be forever grateful for anything you can do for us," Ori replied. They all stood staring and waiting for the boy arrayed in green to respond.

After a few moments, he spoke:

"Bring him out to me, please," he said. Ori and the others carried Pazou's body out to Parelo and laid him down in front of him. Parelo sat down a few feet away from him, but facing him, and crossed his legs. He closed his eyes to channel the power of the ring. The others stood behind him in the distance so not to distract him.

After a few minutes had passed, Parelo's head raised and he opened his eyes and mouth. They were both glowing a bright, emerald green. He raised both his arms, and the earth started to shake and the earth below Pazou began to raise his body up, up into the air. The trees began to give up their roots, and they moved quickly and fluidly, wrapping Pazou's body up into their green, leafy vines. Parelo stood up and the bright, green glow flowed out of Parelo's hands and surrounded Pazou's entire body. He held this position and the glow remained for several minutes, while the others watched in awe. Parelo's face and body began to perspire, and he dropped to his knees, releasing Pazou's body from the glowing energy. Pazou's body remained motionless on top of the pillar of dirt, and the vines held tightly to his frame.

The others, concerned now for Parelo, rushed over to him, taking him by the arms and lifting him to his feet, Jimmy on one side and Ryan on the other. They could tell that Parelo was exhausted from the experience and hoped that he had not been harmed by it. They helped him to the campfire and brought him some water in an ice cup that Zoonee had fashioned for them. Parelo was sweating and feverish to the touch, but he was able to hold and to drink from the ice cup Zoonee was holding for him.

Ori, coming over to him, "Are you alright, Parelo," he asked, worried. "You seemed to have used all your focus and energy to heal Pazou. For that, we are forever in your debt."

Raising his eyes to meet Ori's, "You are very welcome, sir. I owe him life. The process has made me very weak, like nothing I have ever experienced. It was like the ring took a part of me and gave it to him. I must remember this," he smiled. "Can you take me to lie down? I think I need to rest a while."

"Of course, Parelo," answered Ori. Jimmy and Ryan assisted him to a hut, one on each side. Zoonee, feeling bad about her earlier comments to Ori, got up and went over to him. Ori, seeing her, welcomed her with a smile.

"Will Pazou be okay?" she asked softly.

Ori, straight-faced, "I hope so, Zoonee, and I'm sorry for all of this pain. I didn't want Pazou to go alone, but we couldn't risk sending one of you with him. All of you are the key to stopping Gorlev. I hope you believe me and come to understand your importance in this mission." He reached out to her, again, placing one hand on her shoulder. Zoonee, nodded, and then Ori went to the hut to see about the new Ring Bearer.

Jimmy and Ryan came out to see about Zoonee who was standing by the pillar of dirt. Jimmy came up behind her and placed his hands softly on her shoulders. Ryan, who normally teased them, thought it best to say nothing this time.

"That was incredible, huh?" Jimmy asked her. "He used the strength of nature or something to do that. He's gonna be a lot of help defeating Gorlev and his men."

"We're going to kick his butt!" Ryan replied, livid. "He's not going to get away with this, Zoonee." They both looked at Ryan, stunned by his emotional outburst. Jimmy held out his arm and Ryan fist bumped him. The look in their eyes was one of extreme vitriol. They weren't afraid anymore: they were angry. Zoonee, with a puzzled look, followed their lead and let Ryan fist bump her as well. Ryan, realizing that he and Zoonee had just bonded, grinned and nodded his head in approval. Zoonee nodded and smiled back at him.

Back in the hut, Ori watched as Parelo quietly slept. He knew that the ring had powers to perform such miraculous events, but he had never seen one like this exhibited before today. He thought about what it would mean if it actually worked, if it actually cured and saved the life of Pazou. He also wondered what long-term effects it would have on the one who had executed such a daring feat. He wanted to keep a close eye on his new friend, and try to grasp the secret of such a powerful manifestation in order to offer better guidance to Jimmy.

Like the others, he was also angry and wanted to attack and to defeat Gorlev for his crimes against them. But, he knew that Jimmy, Ryan, Zoonee, and Parelo needed battle training. Without it, they would rush into the fight and lose their lives. As much as he desired to defeat Gorlev, he had to do his duty, which was to protect the Ring Bearers at all costs. He knew he could not defeat Gorlev without them, but he also didn't want to have to watch one of them perish at his hands.

Later that evening, Ori came out to warm his hands by the fire and to answer any questions that they might have concerning recent events. But, he felt that it was necessary to keep the conversation lighthearted given their circumstances. He also felt that they needed and deserved a reprieve, a mental break from battle preparation and thoughts of vengeance. He realized that they were only teenagers, and their lives should not always be about preparing for combat or protecting the rings. He knew that he had spent most of his life protecting rings, but he didn't want them to have to make those same sacrifices that he chose to make at their age. He also admired them for their commitment and for their preparation with respect to the challenge that lay ahead of each of them.

Ori, sitting down among them, "How is Pazou?" he asked them. He placed his hands out to warm them by the fire.

Zoonee, answering, "We don't know yet. He's still sleeping. How's the new kid?"

"He's still resting," Ori replied. "I think the process took a lot out of him."

"How did he do that?" Jimmy inquired.

"I imagine that he used all his concentration and energy to communicate with the ring. In essence, the ring is to be used for good, but I've never seen it used in this manner," he paused to reflect, "to heal or to cure someone, though I have heard that it can and has," he admitted. "It takes time to bond with the source of the ring's power." No one spoke for several minutes, and Ori decided to lighten the mood with a story.

"Here's a story for all of you," he said, grinning. "Once there was a family of three: a mother, father, and a son. They all lived out in the wilderness on a mountain. One day the son of the family decided to go exploring and he discovered a small enclave of people near the base of mountain. The people were afraid and on guard because they had never met an outsider. They grabbed him by both arms and locked him away in a hut made of wood."

"Day after day, the guardians of the boy searched for him, never considering that he would have made the journey to the base of the mountain. Then, one night, the rain poured and poured, and the small enclave was not prepared for the flooding that had come with the storm. The boy shouted to them to release him; and the people, having compassion, freed and took him with them, up, up into the mountain. They had lost everything: their homes, their sheep, and their livelihood."

"Eventually, the people came upon the house of the family who had been grief-stricken from the loss of their only child. The men prepared themselves for battle, but the mother and father, having lost everything, too, were also ready. Spears up, the people launched an attack on the family in the house. The man and woman fired back with their guns. The boy, predicting the terrible outcome, ran to the front, in the middle of the conflict. He pleaded with his mother and father, and he pleaded with the indigenous people to stop fighting. Once the smoke cleared, the mother and father realized who the boy was and put down their weapons. Seeing the courage in the foreign boy, the leader of the people commanded his men to stop throwing their spears and firing their arrows."

"The mother and father were so happy that they didn't wait for the people to stop throwing spears and firing their arrows. They came out running to their boy and the boy to them. The men and women of the indigenous people saw the tears and the warmth of their embrace, and they, too, began to hug and to kiss their loved ones. The father and the leader moved cautiously toward one another, but they, too, embraced in peace."

"From that day forth, because of the courage of one boy, the family and the people from the enclave were able to live together in harmony. The boy had shown them that, despite their differences, they still shared many of the same values. The most important one ...being compassion."

Zoonee, seeing a connection, "Parelo showed us compassion by trying to heal Pazou. Jimmy showed a snake compassion by not killing him after he attacked us," she smiled. "Great story, Ori."

Jimmy and Ryan together, "Great story, Ori!" They looked at each other and laughed.

"Jinx," Ryan said to Jimmy, hitting him on the shoulder.

Jimmy teasing, "I'll 'Jinx' you, geek. I'll drown you," he said, wrestling with Ryan.

"I'll throw you into the wind, lover boy," he said, trying to keep Jimmy's arms from clutching his own.

Ori, seeing that his story had its intended effect, decided to get up and to go bed. Zoonee, ignoring the laugher of the teenage boys for a moment, noticed him leaving.

"Good night, Ori," she said, forgiving him.

Ori turning, "Good night, Zoonee."

The boys together, "Good night, Ori!" They said, continuing to horseplay with each other.

Chapter Five
The Best Man

A few days had passed, and the vines magically unraveled from Pazou's frame. He was able to sit up and hang his legs off the pillar of earth. It was about dawn, and Ori was the first one to emerge from his hut to check on Pazou.

Pazou, seeing Ori, "Good morning, Sir," he laughed, picking the remaining leaves off his arms and legs.

Ori, looking up, "Good morning, Pazou," he smiled, waving at him from below. Pazou, looked below, assessing the situation.

"I think I may need some more help from our friends," he smiled, displaying both rows of his teeth. Ori, measuring, decided to wake Zoonee and the boys.

"I'll be right back," he said, and went to get help. Zoonee, excited to hear that Pazou was alive, burst out of the hut.

Zoonee hollering, "Pazou, you're alive! Yay!" she shouted. "I'll get you down!" She stood directly below the pillar; and, using her power, she produced an ice slide to allow Pazou to get down. Pazou slid down the ice slide, and then he wrapped his arms around Zoonee, picking her up.

"I'm so happy to see you again, my child," he said, beaming. The others ran over to him to hug him. "Easy, I'm still not quite well," he admitted.

"I'm glad you're better, Pazou," Jimmy said.

"Me, too, man," Ryan retorted.

"And so am I, friend," Ori stated, grinning.

Pazou noticed that Parelo was running toward him, and he made his way through the others to catch him in the air. "Thank you, my boy," he said, sincerely. "I owe you my life."

"I owed you mine, first," Parelo responded.

"I know that I cannot take the place of Sazzo, but I am here for you if you need me," he said, earnestly. Parelo hugged him again. Zoonee, with tears rolling down her cheeks, came over to Parelo and hugged him as well.

"Thank you, Parelo. You saved my Guardian," she said.

"You are welcome, Zoonee," he replied. The others came over and thanked him, too. They all decided to have a feast to celebrate this miraculous event. Jimmy and Ryan caught the fish, Zoonee procured a beehive and made honey sickles, and Parelo used his powers to find edible berries in the forest. He even used them to bring forth friendly animals for them to pet for the day: an eagle, a fox, and a wolf. They were all amazed by his abilities and his training with the Emerald Ring of The Earth.

They all quickly began to like the dark-haired, fifteen-year-old, wearing green garments. They joined each other in a game of sorts, displaying their powers as if they were fireworks being set off in July. Jimmy created a water spout in the center of the clearing, bringing some of the river water out onto the dry land. Zoonee, creatively, made an ice funnel for it, and Parelo brought flowers to the surface around it. Ryan, adding the finishing touch, twirled the water into the air, causing it to twist for a few moments.

In the background, Ori and Pazou witnessed the majesty of these exhibitions. More important, however, Ori observed the way in which they worked together as a team. He surmised that, if they could do this against Gorlev, then they could win the battle of the rings. They

89

both applauded and verbally praised them for their performances.

The next day, battle training began. Ori and Pazou were both outside assisting the Ring Bearers and Ryan, the lone Guardian apprentice. Jimmy was the first one up to face Ori. He produced water balls and threw them, one at a time, at Ori. Ori, being ready, twirled his staff, blocking and casting them aside into the bushes and into a large boulder.

It was Zoonee's turn. She produced multiple, large ice balls and sent them flying at Pazou. Pazou, as Ori had done, twirled his staff, dispensing with the ice balls. Zoonee, displaying her consternation, moved out of the way to allow Parelo to have his turn. Parelo, being fifteen, and having been trained for a longer time period than the rest of them, made the ground shake, causing it to raise and to split in places, forcing Pazou to retreat to another area. They all saw this and praised Parelo for his ingenuity.

Ori challenged Parelo. He used his staff to try to knock Parelo down, but Parelo used a thick wall of dirt to block the strong gust of wind. He then summoned a golden eagle to fly down and snatch away Ori's staff. Ori, cleverly, used his cane to temporarily blind the eagle, causing the eagle to drop his staff, and then he used it to throw Parelo into the bushes behind him.

Jimmy, coming over to help him up, "Don't worry about it," he said, "It's tough to beat Ori."

Parelo, proudly, "I don't need your help," he scoffed. "I can do it myself." He got up and narrowed his eyes at Jimmy. Parelo stood up as Jimmy walked away. Jimmy was confused by Parelo's reaction to his help. Parelo could see that Ori was waiting for him to counter with something, so he summoned a gray wolf from out of the woods. The wolf snarled at Ori. Ori, not panicking, but also not wanting to harm the wolf, accepted defeat.

"Very good, Parelo," he said. "You have won this round." Parelo turned and responded with a smirk toward Jimmy, not Ori. Then, he turned to the wolf and commanded him to leave the campsite. Jimmy, not knowing exactly what to think about Parelo's reactions, decided not to say anything all. He was perplexed by Parelo's responses to him.

Ryan, having observed everything, "Perhaps he's just really competitive," he said in an aside to Jimmy. Jimmy didn't say anything; he just simply nodded to Ryan. He turned to watch Zoonee congratulating Parelo on a successful first day of training. The two of them walked off together to the fire pit. Something inside Jimmy told him that this turn of events had to do with more than just competition.

That night, Jimmy listened to Zoonee and Parelo share their family history, the good and bad, and their similarities with one another, just as they had done the first time they had met. Jimmy admitted to himself that he was a smidge jealous of the pair, but he also knew that it was good for Zoonee to make other friends. She had grown up in relative isolation with few contacts, and he could see that getting to know others meant the world to her. He cared for her and did not want to stand in her way.

As he watched her, he smiled to himself because he knew it was making her happy. Zoonee, catching his glance and smile, smiled to herself as well. She had not forgotten about Jimmy.

As the night was coming to an end, Jimmy finished his meal and made his way to his hut with Ryan.

"Good night, Zoonee. Good night, Parelo," he said. Parelo looked up at him and then down again, not responding in kind.

Zoonee, noticing, but not commenting, "Good night, Jimmy," she said, affectionately watching him enter his hut for the night.

The next day, training continued. Ori began by knocking Jimmy backwards with the wind generated by his staff. Parelo, sitting on a large rock beside Zoonee, snickered at him as he was getting up off the ground. Zoonee, once again, observed Parelo's reaction, but didn't say anything. Once on his feet, Jimmy, concentrating as hard as possible, created a massive sheet of water above Ori's head that seemed to follow his movements. Ori, realizing he could not avoid the water, nodded to Jimmy, and he moved the water off to the side and let it fall on some trees.

Ori, acknowledging, "Good work, Jimmy. Keep it up."

"Thank you, Ori," he replied, breathing a sigh of relief. He looked at Ryan and Zoonee. They both clapped for him. Parelo, seeing Zoonee clapping, glowered at Jimmy. Jimmy, sensing that this situation had something to do with Zoonee, looked down and away. But, he knew that he would have to confront him, sooner or later.

It was Ryan's turn. He had been using Ori's staff to train, but he knew that he would eventually need his own. He held the staff in the air above him, admiring the azure-like gem encased at the top. He brought it down to ready himself for battle.

Pazou was awaiting an offensive move from him. Ryan, twirling the staff once in his hands, used the staff to scoop up Pazou and flip him over to the ground. Pazou, reacting with great control, landed on his feet and then countered with the same move, causing Ryan to fall on his backside. Ryan jumped up on his feet and lifted a rock up and hurled it at Pazou's chest. Pazou, seeing it coming, stepped aside to avoid its impact and flung the rock back at Ryan, striking him in his right arm.

Pazou, impressed by his growth, "Well, done, my young friend," he said, bowing.

Ryan, grateful, but distraught, "Not good enough, though," he admitted.

Pazou, smiling, "I have been a Guardian for a long time now. But, you will surpass me, one day." Ryan bowed to him and took his seat. Zoonee came over to him to ice the bruise he had sustained from the training sequence.

Knowing it was his turn, Parelo stepped up to face Ori. Parelo had gotten the best of Ori the first time and was planning to do the same this time. He saw a tree on one side of the clearing, so he made one of the roots from the tree free itself. He tried to wrap the legs of Ori with the roots, but Ori blocked them with his staff. The roots twisted and pulled on Ori's staff until he was forced to let the roots have it. Parelo had disarmed Ori and won again.

"Excellent, Parelo. Your fighting skills are advanced," he affirmed. Parelo looked around to see Zoonee and Ryan clapping their hands in recognition. Jimmy clapped his hands gently, but Parelo gazed at him with contempt.

Pointing his finger at Jimmy,

"I want to battle Jimmy," he said to Ori.

Sensing animosity, "We are not really at that stage," Ori pointed out.

"I won't hurt him," Parelo replied, arrogantly. Ori, looking over at Jimmy, realizing that he had just been challenged, motioned to him to come forth.

"Okay, Parelo. Jimmy, spar with Parelo," he ordered. Jimmy, a little apprehensive, agreed and walked over to meet Parelo's smug grin and eager eyes. Jimmy prepared himself, still unsure of Parelo's intentions or his feelings toward him.

Parelo, eyes glowing green, caused a vine from four different trees to snatch Jimmy's four limbs and pull them to where his body was in the shape of an X. Jimmy, straining, could not free himself from the vines, and Parelo, grinning, assumed that he had won.

"Are you ready to accept defeat? Are you ready to admit that I am the best in this group?" Parelo asked, smugly. The rest of the group were surprised by Parelo's words and tone and were not sure how to respond. They watched Jimmy struggle, hoping he would free himself from the vines.

But, Jimmy, relaxing and looking up in Parelo's direction, eyes glowing blue, caused water to appear in front of Parelo. The water wrapped him up into a cocoon and began to circle him with increasing speed and force.

After a few minutes, Parelo lost his concentration and the vines freed Jimmy. But, Jimmy did not release Parelo, and he began to spin around with the watery vortex.

Ori, astonished, but calmly, "Okay, Jimmy, that's enough." Jimmy, listening and obeying Ori's instructions, immediately caused the water to begin its dissipation. Parelo, extremely disoriented and dizzy, fell down onto the ground.

No one clapped this time. They were all too amazed by the power Jimmy had released on Parelo and taken aback by his words to Jimmy. Ori and Pazou went over to Parelo to help him get to his feet. Parelo refused their help. He sat on the ground with his knees up and his head down, trying to recover from the dizziness. Jimmy, weakened by this display of force, fell to his knees. Zoonee and Ryan went over to aid him.

"That's enough sparring for today," Ori stated. "We will continue again tomorrow." Once on his feet, Parelo leered at Jimmy for a few moments, and then headed toward the camp.

Back at camp, Jimmy visited with the others, but Parelo kept his distance. He didn't speak to anyone, though Pazou tried to cheer him up, sensing his disappointment.

Pazou, aside to Parelo, "You did well today. There is no shame. Jimmy just did a little better. Your power is great, my young friend," he said, reassuringly. Parelo didn't lift his head or speak. He was disappointed, jealous, and desired vindication. He swore secretly to himself that he would eventually have it.

The next morning, the sky was dark with ominous clouds. Everyone could tell that a storm was about to let loose upon the clearing.

Zoonee observing, "I guess we won't be sparring today, huh Ori?"

Ori, grinning, "No, I don't think we will today. But, we will still train." Zoonee and the others looked at him, puzzled.

Ori, explaining, "When the storm begins, be sure to follow my instructions," he requested. A few moments later the clouds dumped its contents upon them in the form of copious amounts of piercing rain. The teens turned and bolted for the huts—

"Stop," Ori ordered. "Jimmy, use the ring to redirect the rain." As obvious as it was, Jimmy didn't realize at the time that he could manipulate the rain. He began to focus on what he desired, his eyes glowing, and he redirected the rain, causing it to take a different path to the ground away from the campsite.

"Now, Parelo," Ori directed, "Give us some shelter." Parelo smirked at the boys. He used a few trees, vines, and roots to create a canopy above them. He even used the foliage to weave a small door.

Ori, turning his attention to Zoonee, "I need you to freeze the surface of the river so that it doesn't flood the forest or the clearing." Zoonee understood. She and the boys went to the training area. Once there, they ran to the cliff overlooking the green river. Zoonee motioned to them to stand back, so she could concentrate. In a dazzling display of power, she froze the entire body of water in a matter of seconds.

The boys couldn't believe their eyes.

"That was so, so rad," Ryan commented.

Jimmy laughing, "You're nuts, dude."

Parelo grinned at Zoonee but refused to acknowledge Ryan and Jimmy.

When they had all returned to the campsite, they went into the new shelter and sat down around Ori, which formed a circle.

Ori, looking up to speak, "You see," addressing them all, "...your powers are not only for battle. You can use them to survive or to help others. But, always remember, two Ring Bearers are better than one. You must see past yourself: your fears, your jealousy, and your desires. Your purpose is much larger than yourself," he stated, as if he were a wise old sage. Everyone in the group looked up and nodded, except for Parelo.

That night, everyone was sitting around the fire as the storm had come to an end. They decided to come out of the shelter and to go into their huts to sleep. Zoonee, Jimmy, and Ryan stood outside talking.

"I wonder if we are ready to face our enemy," Zoonee said, concerned. Jimmy and Ryan glanced at each other, and then they turned back to Zoonee. Neither of them really knew the right answer.

"All we can really do is our best, right?" Jimmy replied after a long pause. Ryan nodded in approval, but his eyes displayed apprehension.

Suddenly, two wolves emerged from the clearing, growling menacingly. They trotted slowly up to the three teens. The teens stood still, frozen with fear. The wolves came within a few feet of them and then stopped short.

"Ah, I guess this answers your question," a voice said from behind them. The wolves stopped growling and sat down in front of them. The three teens turned to see Parelo walking toward them, his eyes glowing bright green. He walked straight up to the wolves and kneeled down to pet them.

"If you are afraid of a couple wolves, then how will you defeat Gorlev and his henchmen?" he asked in a dubious tone. Eyes still glowing, he induced the wolves to go back into the woods. Then, he stood up curling his lip at each of them.

"Did you call these wolves out here?" Zoonee asked, glowering at Parelo.

"So what if I did? What are you *three* going to do about it?" Parelo sneered. They narrowed their eyes at him but said nothing.

"That's what I thought," he said, threateningly, staring at each one of them in turn. Then, he casually made his way back to his hut where he slept alone.

"Well, so much for teamwork," Ryan responded, grinning. Zoonee and Jimmy tried, but failed to smile. They knew that they would need Parelo to defeat Gorlev, but they now questioned his devotion to their cause.

"What do you think his problem is?" Zoonee asked, looking for answers in the eyes of the boys. "Before the training, he was fine," she added.

"Bad hair day," Ryan replied, to which they both laughed. What they didn't know was that Parelo was listening, and he clinched his fists in anger. He was determined to show them his strength, and he was waiting for the right moment to exact revenge for what he considered contemptuous banter.

The next morning the sparring continued. This time Zoonee and Jimmy would spar, and then Ryan and Parelo would be pitted against each other. Zoonee and Jimmy squared off ready for action. Jimmy, grinning, created a ball of water and sent it spinning at an unknown speed at Zoonee's chest. Zoonee retaliated by forming an ice shield, which blocked the initial force of the water ball, but it still caused Zoonee to lose her balance and to fall back to the ground.

Jimmy, teasing, "You okay there, girly?" Zoonee got to her feet quickly, trying to look serious, but she was too amused by his query.

"Fine," she remarked, and then she sent an ice ball soaring toward his chest. Jimmy, caught off guard by the blazing speed of the ice ball, was forced to dodge it. Ori looked at him, confused by his passive reaction. Jimmy just shrugged his shoulders and began his next assault. He sent a small wave up over Zoonee, to which she calmly and strategically turned into ice. She turned the wave to face Jimmy, and she ran up the wave leaping into the air and flipped to land behind him. When Jimmy turned around to face her, she froze his feet, causing him to fall to ground.

Again, Jimmy turned and looked at Ori's puzzled face.

"Okay, so *ice* girl may be my weakness," he suggested, half-smiling. Zoonee came over proudly and broke up the ice at his feet.

"Good job, *ice* girl," Jimmy said, blushing.

Zoonee teasing, "You, too, *water* boy." She smiled and patted him on the shoulder, and then they took their seats by Ori and Pazou.

Next up was Ryan and Parelo. Parelo starred Ryan down, and Ryan waivered a bit, but tried to stare him down, too. Abruptly, Parelo hurled a fallen tree trunk at Ryan. Ryan gasped and ducked to allow the trunk to fly over him. Ori gazed at Parelo, but he didn't speak or deter him. In response, Ryan twirled the staff and sent a dust tornado toward him. Parelo cartwheeled to his left to escape the swirling dust. As soon as he made it to his feet, his eyes began glowing and a panther leaped from the bushes and headed straight for Ryan. Jimmy, standing, immediately sent a wave of water to swallow up the panther. The panther whined and ran back into the woods.

Ryan, irate, "Are you trying to kill me?" he asked furiously. Jimmy moved toward Parelo, but Pazou put out his staff to restrain him. They all gazed at Parelo, trying to understand his motives. Parelo glanced at them and then left for the clearing.

"What is wrong with him? He could've killed Ryan," Jimmy inquired, vexed. Ori and Pazou looked at each other as if the one knew what the other was thinking, but neither spoke openly.

"I think that is enough for today," Ori said, contemplatively. Then they all began to head back to the campsite.

Later that evening, they could hear Pazou and Parelo speaking loudly to each other.

"I didn't ask for any of this!" Parelo stated, angrily.

"I know. You were chosen for this destiny. We all were, and we all have to accept it. It's who we are in this world," Pazou explained.

"I don't accept it!" Parelo retorted, emphatically. "And, I don't have to be here among these *weak* people."

Pazou, instructively, "They are not *weak*. It is never *weak* to be yourself. You should be proud to be counted among those who are *like* you."

Parelo, stubbornly, "I do not! Now, leave me alone." Pazou, seeing that his words had fallen by the wayside, bowed morosely and left him. Jimmy and Ryan couldn't believe what they had heard, and they discussed it quietly before going to sleep.

Ryan, uneasy, "I think he tried to kill me, today." Jimmy looked across the inside of the hut at him. He was trying to make sense of the situation. He knew there was friction between them, but he didn't quite understand the reasons.

Ryan was awaiting a response.

"I don't think he was trying to kill you. But, he may have been sending us a message. He definitely doesn't like me; he may even hate me," Jimmy said, after some reflection.

"But, why? We are all on the same side." Ryan replied, befuddled.

"I know. It doesn't make any sense. I think we should talk to Ori about it, tomorrow," Jimmy decided. Ryan consented, and they both closed their eyes to rest.

Chapter Six
The New Guardian

As soon as the sun had come up, the boys made a b-line for Ori, who was discussing something with Pazou and Zoonee in the shelter that Parelo had created. They burst in to see what was amiss and to question Ori about Parelo's behavior.

"Come in, gentlemen, you two are right on time for this conversation," Ori said. They could tell that something was wrong. Ori was trying too hard to be amiable. Jimmy and Ryan noticed that Parelo was not among them, and Zoonee did not greet them as they entered. They sat down to listen.

"Parelo is gone. He left last night through the portal at the beginning of the clearing. We don't know where he has gone, and we don't expect him to return. It's disappointing, but we have to plan without him, now," he stated in a matter of fact tone. The boys could sense the tension in the shelter. They knew that this was not a good omen, and they also knew that Parelo was a valuable weapon and ally against their foe.

Pazou added a few words: "His heart has taken him down a different path, but we must continue down our own." Ori tried to smile fully at Pazou's turning of phrases, but he seemed to falter. For the first time, he was having a difficult time being his cheerful, positive self. The boys observed this abnormality, but they needed to understand Parelo's decision and how it would effect their purpose.

Jimmy, interrupting the silence, "But, why would he do this? We need to know. Did we do something wrong?" Ori took a deep breath, and began to explain.

"Not all Ring Bearers are good, Jimmy. Not all of them are dedicated to our cause. Having said that, there could be a number of reasons. Perhaps he is in agony over the death of his Guardian. Or, perhaps the problem is envy," he said, making eye contact with Jimmy.

"Why would he be--?" Jimmy asked, oblivious.

"It is not certain, Mr. Jimmy," Pazou interjected, "but we believe he may be envious of your friendship with Zoonee. But, as Ori has said, there could be many unknown reasons." Zoonee looked up at Jimmy, and Jimmy looked back into her shiny, dark eyes. They both realized that there could be a stitch of truth in Pazou's words. They were also both ashamed because they believed they had caused Parelo's departure. They both looked down at the ground.

Pazou, seeing their reactions, said, "Do not blame yourselves. It is very hard to fight against the natural procession of things. Parelo made his decision. Now we must stand by ours."

Jimmy nodded in agreement, and the other teenagers followed suit. If anything, they were now more determined to complete their mission to stop their enemy and to save the known world.

Over the next several days, they were all focused and trained diligently. The congratulations and giddiness were placed on hold. They could not afford any mistakes now that Parelo was gone and had taken his ring and amazing abilities with him. They were all getting closer to mastering their chosen powers and becoming one with the essence of their rings.

"Okay, let's see what you've got, you two," Ori said, challenging Jimmy and Zoonee.

No more games...no more holding back. This is for real, thought Jimmy. He could tell by the expression on

Zoonee's face that they were like-minded on this issue. Zoonee, her ring and eyes glowing, sent four deadly ice spikes at Jimmy's figure. Not panicking or dodging, but holding his ground, Jimmy created a force of water so great that it exploded in a "Whoosh!" out of thin air, which diverted the spikes into the air and caused them to land at different locations, piercing the soft ground and breaking on large rocks.

The spectators marveled at the exhibition of controlled power. The two combatants did not smile amicably. They bowed to each other formally out of respect and sat down. Ryan and Pazou were up next. Pazou twirled his staff beside him and generated enough wind to lift himself up into the air toward Ryan. Ryan did the same, and they met in the air with their staffs colliding like thunder, as they fenced in mid-air for a few moments, and then twirled themselves back to the ground. Everyone could see that Ryan had nearly mastered his art. Though they were impressed, and desired to applaud him, they chose to stay silent and focused.

That night Pazou invited Ryan into his shelter to speak with him about his level of attainment. Ryan came into his hut and Pazou motioned for him to sit down. Pazou unrolled some wrappings that seemed to hold a long, straight object. It was a Guardian staff. It was the staff of the former Emerald Ring Guardian. Ryan could easily tell that it belonged to Parelo's former mentor, who had been burned to death in an unmerciless way by Gorlev. Ryan's eyes lit up when he saw the magnificent emerald encased at the top of the staff. It glistened in the darkness of the shelter, though Pazou's cane offered plenty of light.

"It is speaking to you, Mr. Ryan. It has chosen you. You are now its new master. But, you must swear the Guardian Oath. Repeat after me," he requested.

I swear allegiance and unconditional loyalty to the gods who forged this staff for the purpose of protecting and guiding the Ring Bearer, whose element it upholds, until my death.

Ryan didn't hesitate, and he did as Pazou instructed. He made the solemn vow...and was now a Guardian of the Emerald Ring of the Earth. He knew what this meant before he took the vow. He knew that he was now obligated to Parelo for the rest of his life. He graciously took Sazzo's staff and cane, and he thanked Pazou.

Pazou continued. "We must not give up on Parelo. He is one of us...he is just confused and suffering. It is not easy to lose a mentor. You may be Parelo's only hope."

Ryan slowly nodded his head. He suddenly experienced an overwhelming desire to aid Parelo, and he also empathized with him, having lost his father early in his life.

Ryan, committed, "I will do everything I can to bring Parelo back to us...and everything I can to support him once he dedicates himself to the cause."

Pazou smiled and bowed to him. Relaxing, Ryan had a question for Pazou.

"Where are you *from*, exactly?"

Pazou, amused at the boy's fickleness, but inspired by his dedication:

"I am half African and half Chilean. My father was a geologist researcher from South Africa and my mother was Chilean, like Zoonee's mother and father. I was born in Antarctica. My native languages are Spanish, English and Afrikaans. My mother, father, and the school taught me," he elaborated.

"Oh, okay, that explains a lot. You got an accent that no one has been able to identify yet, huh?" he asked, chuckling to himself, as Pazou grinned back at him. Pazou appreciated Ryan's sense of humor, and he believed it was a gift from Gelos, the Greek god of laughter, who had granted it to them during these perilous times.

Ryan's forehead wrinkled, and he became more serious.

"Will Ori be okay with this? I thought I was going to be his successor," he reasoned.

"You are Ori's apprentice. He has trained you very well. That does not mean that you will take his place. Ori understands this, and he will be very proud when he hears," Pazou explained.

This was enough for Ryan, and he proudly stood up on his feet.

"Good night, Pazou...and thanks," he said earnestly.

"Good night, young Guardian."

The following morning, as Pazou had predicted, Ori was truly proud of Ryan. He embraced him affectionately and then introduced him as the new Guardian of the

Emerald Ring of Earth. Of course, there was the obvious issue, which everyone knew, but they were exceedingly happy for Ryan.

That night Ryan asked Jimmy and Zoonee to meet with him once Ori and Pazou had fallen asleep. They met far enough away from the huts so that they couldn't be overheard. Jimmy and Zoonee could see the anxiousness on his hairless visage.

"Okay, so I know I just became a Guardian, but I have this uncontrollable desire to help Parelo. I can even sense his location. He's in Europe. Germany, I think, and I'm pretty sure he's in trouble," he said, intently.

Jimmy looked at Zoonee, and they were on the same page, thinking the same way. They knew what Ryan wanted from them.

"You want us to go with you to rescue Parelo?" he guessed. Ryan looked at Zoonee and then back at Jimmy. He nodded.

"If he's in Germany, then you know who has him," Ryan stated, nervously. "We have to find him and bring him back."

Zoonee, now grasping his meaning,

"It's suicide," Zoonee whispered. "We need Ori and Pazou for a rescue attempt," she added, in an effort to dissuade them from their current state of mind.

"No, no we don't. I'm sure I can find him," Ryan argued, "and they will never see it coming...It will work."

"What if he decides not to come back with us?" Jimmy asked. "You heard what Pazou and Ori told us...not to mention the fact that I'm pretty sure he tried to kill both of us."

"He's just in pain; and he is confused. That's all. I can talk him into it," Ryan retorted. Jimmy looked at Zoonee and then back at Ryan. He believed that he needed to support his best friend, but he also knew this task was dangerous.

"Okay, I'll do it, but we have to make it quick," he said. Zoonee sighed, but nodded in agreement. She was a part of the team, something larger than herself, and she believed in her friends.

"Wait! How do you know where he is?" Jimmy questioned. Zoonee glanced to Jimmy and then back Ryan.

"Don't you remember what Ori told us when we signed up for this? Ori said that a Guardian's staff has the power to find another Guardian, or find the ring *that* Guardian protects," he reminded him. "The power of the element speaks to us from the staff. That's how I know where to go and how to find Parelo. We saw Ori do it at the German home," Ryan elaborated, trying to facilitate Jimmy's memory.

Jimmy, remembering,

"Oh...right, okay. Let's go," Jimmy conceded. Then the three of them moved to the opening of the clearing to the portal that was only marked by two rock pillars on both sides with ancient, Greek markings.

"Ready?" Ryan asked them.

"No, not really," remarked Zoonee. "But let's do it, guys." Jimmy nodded and took a deep breath.

"In the name of the gods, give us Guardians passage!" Ryan proclaimed.

Chapter Seven
The Risky Rescue

It was dark when the teenagers arrived in Germany, but they weren't exactly sure where. They knew that they were in a field, and a light pole allowed them to see cattle drinking from a trough in the distance underneath a tree. Further in the distance, they could see what appeared to be an old barn with a light on inside, and a house above it on top of a hill. The house had several lights on inside and looked quite large to them. It was too dark for them to observe its architecture or color.

The teens moved closer to the barn, and Ryan tapped his supernatural cane to provide them with more light.

"I think he's in the house," Ryan said, noticing that the crystal at the top of his staff was glowing. The closer he came to finding Parelo, the brighter it seemed to glow.

As they moved closer to the house, while trying to stay hidden from anyone inside, they could see people moving past the window drapes. Then, two shadows emerged from the doorway of the house carrying flashlights. The men seemed to be walking toward them;

the teens braced themselves for battle, but the men turned and headed for the barn.

Ryan observed the movement of the flashlights.

"No, not in the house, that's where they are keeping Parelo," Ryan asserted, pointing his staff in the direction of the barn. They all turned their attention to the barn. They knew that they had to make a move soon.

"Look, there's a window on one side of the barn at the top. You and Zoonee can go that way while I distract the guards," suggested Jimmy.

"How do we know that there aren't more of them inside?" Ryan asked, looking at Jimmy.

Jimmy swallowed hard before speaking.

"I won't move to the front of the barn until you two have had plenty of time to get ready. That way, if there are more, then you guys can get them while I concentrate on those two," he carefully explained. "Either way, we have the element of surprise."

"Good idea," Zoonee whispered. Ryan nodded under the dim light of his cane.

Moments later, Zoonee and Ryan crept toward the barn. The closer they came to the barn window, the easier it was for them to see that the barn was old and painted red. Zoonee quietly created an ice latter and slowly went up into the barn first. Ryan followed, trying not to slip and fall from the ice. Once in, Ryan placed his hands in his pockets to thaw. They were both perched on top of a wooden platform and could see hay in front of them. They surmised that they were on a hay loft, and they decided to move closer to the front to see down to the bottom of barn.

Looking down from behind some bales of hay, they could see the men talking to someone. It was Parelo. He was chained to a post, and the men appeared to be baiting him. Parelo, livid, tried to break the chains, but to no avail.

A few minutes passed...

Bam!

Suddenly, Jimmy burst through the barn doors and sent one ball of water at each of the two guards, disarming them. Ryan hit one with a large hay bale from the loft, and Zoonee quickly froze them where they stood.

Parelo watched incredulously as Ryan, twirling the staff, flew down to his aid, and Zoonee slid down an ice slide to land right in front of him. Jimmy, who had learned to shoot guns from his grandfather, picked up one of the Lugers.

Bang!

With one shot, and everyone staring at him in disbelief, Jimmy freed Parelo from his chains. They grabbed him, and ran out the front door to the portal beyond the tree, marked by two ancient posts.

Hearing the gunshot, more men, along with Gorlev and another, ran down the doorsteps of the house. The two henchmen fired their guns; but, Gorlev and the other unrecognizable man, stood back and did not pursue them.

Once they reached the portal, Ryan recited the ancient words, and they teleported back to the edge of the clearing.

Once there, Parelo lowered his eyes and head and came over to them.

"*Gracias, amigo,*" he said, earnestly. "I'm sorry about everything." He offered his hand to Jimmy, who smiled, and shook it.

"It's all good, man," he said, forgiving him. "Glad your back." Parelo looked to Ryan, and then he looked at the staff and immediately understood.

"*Gracias, amigo*," he repeated to Ryan. "I guess you are my new Guardian." Ryan went over to Parelo and hugged him.

"'Till death, man," he responded. Parelo turned and bowed to Zoonee.

"*Gracias, mi hermanita*," he said, reaching out to embrace Zoonee as his sister.

"*De nada, hermano mayor*," retorted Zoonee, accepting Parelo's apology and embrace.

Parelo, facing all of them, "*Mi familia*," he said, smiling appreciatively.

Ryan, grinning, "Okay, English, please." They laughed until they saw Ori and Pazou hurrying toward them. Then they all became silent as they stood together, awaiting their punishment.

"How do you say, 'Oh crap!' in Spanish?" whispered Jimmy.

"Oh, *mierda*," Parelo whispered back, chuckling to himself.

"Good to know," muttered Ryan.

Ori and Pazou were visibly concerned.

"Are you guys alright?" Ori questioned them, extremely frazzled. "We have been looking all over for you three. We were about to teleport to Germany in hopes of finding you there. It's what our powers told us."

"We had to get Parelo back, Ori," Jimmy answered, softly.

"It was my—," Ryan began.

"No! It was my fault," Parelo interjected. "I wanted revenge, and I wanted to prove myself, so I went after Gorlev. But, when I got to Germany, there was this dark man who had a purple ring. He used it on me...to control me. He used it to make me give up my ring." Parelo lowered his head as he finished speaking. Ori turned to Pazou before speaking. Their eyes displayed worry.

"I understand why you all did this, but it's dangerous for you to make decisions like this on your own, especially when they are whimsical," Ori cautioned. "Now, Gorlev has two more rings. By going there, you risked your lives, and you risked losing your rings as well...If what Parelo says is true, then the man is the Ring Bearer of the Amethyst Ring of Dominion, which means he can control you if you have a moment of weakness."

Ori turned back to Parelo.

"Your weakness is either your desire for swift justice, or it's your pride," he explained. "You must be patient--this is a major setback. Now we must plan differently." The teens didn't have any words, and their heads hung somberly, eyeing the ground below.

His face softened. "Having said that, you did well. None of you were harmed, and you were willing to sacrifice yourselves to bring back one of us. You placed our cause before yourselves, and you came together as one. Remember: This is the only way we can win this battle."

Ori didn't want to divulge all the details, but he knew they were no longer safe. He believed that Gorlev would come for them at any moment. So, over the next several days, Ori and Pazou began training them to meditate to strengthen their minds, will, and concentration. He taught them to quiet their minds and to focus on one object, blocking out everything else.

Pazou, calmly instructing, "Focus on your breathing. Think of only one thing," he would say. Ori and Pazou had them meditate for several hours each day, and then they sparred later in the afternoon.

Ori knew that they didn't have much time, so he began working on a plan for the arrival of Gorlev and the Ring Bearer, which he believed was somehow being manipulated by him. He considered the irony for a second. *If the Ring Bearer wasn't being coerced, then he had been bribed or promised something in return for his cooperation*, Ori thought to himself. He also knew that Gorlev only needed three more rings to achieve his fiendish goal.

"Okay, today we are going to work on a strategy to defeat Gorlev. I don't know when he is coming after us, but he's definitely coming," Ori stated, looking around at all of them. "Here is the plan that Pazou and I have outlined using these sticks and rocks." Ori and Pazou went over the details of a plan that they believed would force Gorlev to at least surrender and to leave the clearing, giving them enough time to escape.

That night, Jimmy rehearsed the plan in his mind, as Ori had instructed. They all had participated in setting traps and alarms around the clearing. Once a trap or an alarm was triggered, then they were to head to a certain post to ready themselves for battle. Jimmy believed that he was now ready, but there was still some anxiety. He hoped that he would not have to kill someone, even if he or she was trying to kill him. He wasn't sure he could do it.

Chapter Eight
The First Test

It was just before dawn when...

Crunch! *Crunch*! *Crunch*!

That was the sound that started it all...Someone had set off one of the alarms. They heard another one set off:

"Ow!" someone hollered, just outside the huts.

Everyone leaped out of their slumber and ran to their positions. The battle had begun.

Whoosh! This was the sound the fire made as Gorlev showered their huts and the shelter with flaming balls, setting them ablaze.

Bang! *Bang*! *Bang*! Bullets could be heard all around them. Ori and Pazou twirled their bullet proof staffs with so much centripetal force that the bullets could not hit their marks. Then, as the men paused to reload, Ori and Pazou sent them flying into the vegetation which encircled the clearing.

Zoonee jumped out from behind a tree and froze two of the men solid. Gorlev, seeing her, sent three fire balls toward her, but Jimmy shielded her with a wall of water, soaking up the flames. Gorlev turned his attention to Jimmy and created a roller coaster of fire, which he sent straight at him. Jimmy quickly produced a round shield of water to block the lava hot blaze, but the fire hit the water with such force that he was unable to keep from being burned by some of the flames.

"Ow!" Jimmy cried, feeling the burning sensations.

Zoonee, freezing the soaring bullets from another gunman, turned back to Gorlev for a moment. She sent a beam of ice his way, but he consumed it with a shield of fire and a sinister sneer on his face. Zoonee began to panic, as Gorlev regrouped for an assault on her.

"Now!" cried Ryan. Ryan had been hiding behind a boulder in the vegetation surrounding the campsite. He leaped out from behind it and produced a small, spinning funnel of debris in Gorlev's direction.

Gorlev turned into the small vortex created by Ryan's staff, which pushed him into the grass to the edge of the clearing beneath a large tree. Parelo, hiding among the branches of the tree just above him, cut away a net made from tree root that engulfed Gorlev. They knew this wouldn't hold him, but they thought it would buy them some time, if they needed it—and it did...

Zoonee froze the stunned Gorlev, but he had already begun rendering fire. It would only be a matter of seconds before he would be free again. Jimmy and Ryan came up beside Zoonee. They turned to see Ori and Pazou coming toward them. Pazou had been shot in the arm, and Ori had been shot in the shoulder. But, they were able to knock the men unconscious, sending them flying into trees and rocks. Parelo climbed down the tree to join them. All they had to worry about now was Gorlev, who was standing and gazing at them. Fire formed from the tips of his fingers— and his malicious eyes glowed a fiery orange.

Just then, a man stepped forth through the portal. He was a dark man, like Pazou, only taller, and he was bearing the Amethyst Ring of Dominion. He was also arrayed in black with a purple sash and a red Igbo hat. His eyes glowed violet, and he made all of them—Ori, Pazou, Zoonee, Jimmy, Ryan, and Parelo—kneel to the power of the purple ring. All of them had grimaces on their faces, trying to fight the force that had them. Gorlev, thinking he had won, let down his guard to free his frozen soldiers, while the tall man, glowing bright purple, stood in front of them. He moved his head from side to side, observing each of them. He assessed the volition of each one, trying to decide who he could manipulate with his power.

After a few moments, the Ring Bearer spoke to Parelo:

"Come, my child," he said in a fatherly tone of voice. Parelo, not being able to resist, got to his feet and walked to his side.

"Parelo, No!" Ryan yelled. But, it was useless. Parelo peered back at them as if he no longer knew them.

"Now," began Gorlev, "Make the girl come forth to join us." The dark man turned his attention to Zoonee. Zoonee began to fight harder, crying, wincing in mental anguish. She got to one knee...

Suddenly, Ori and Pazou sprung to their feet. They both used their staffs to throw the two men over to the portal. They were all freed. Gorlev glanced in disbelief at the Ring Bearer, and then they got to their feet and ran for the portal. The men who had regained consciousness escaped...all but one.

"Capture that man! We need him," instructed
Ori. Parelo ran the man down, swiping his feet out from
under him, causing him to fall forward into the
ground. Then, he pounced on the man, pulling one of his
arms behind his back, ready to break it.

"No, don't hurt him. Just hold him," Ori
said. Because of his shoulder, Ori asked Jimmy and Ryan
to help carry the man to the nearest tree and to strap him to
it. Zoonee attended to the wounds of Pazou and
Ori. Zoonee cleaned and numbed the wounds, and gave
them some Olive-Leaf Tea, a gift from Athena, to drink to
relax them. She removed the bullets from their wounds. It
was a painstaking procedure, but they knew loss of blood
and infection were worse. She bandaged their wounds with
eggs and honey, and then the teens built another shelter for
all of them.

Ori knew that they had defeated Gorlev and his men
this time. Ori also knew it was only because Gorlev and
the Ring Bearer had underestimated their training. They
would be more prepared the next time they encountered
each other.

Ori believed that it was their turn to strike and that
they would need to leave the familiarity of the haven for

Guardians as soon as their wounds had healed. He also believed that they needed to attempt to communicate secretly with the Amethyst Ring Bearer in order to sway his allegiance. *If they could accomplish that feat, then they might stand a chance of recovering Parelo's ring and defeating Gorlev without injury*, Ori thought to himself, while lying down in the makeshift shelter.

Even though Ori had been hurt, he could not give up and he could not fail to stop Gorlev.

Alone in the forest, Jimmy attended to his wounds as best he could because he knew Zoonee was busy aiding Ori and Pazou. He had learned a few things about the plant life around him from her and Ori, so he knew where to go to find some Snapdragon flowers for his burns.

This was the first time in his life that he was actually hurt physically. While dressing his wounds, he realized how much worse his injuries could have been. He remembered that he had always had his mother to care for him when he had bruised or scratched himself while playing outside in their yard or trying to ramp his bicycle over a small puddle of water. This was really the first time he had ever had to care for himself. In a way, he felt sad by it, but in another way, he felt proud, independent, and strong—like a man. He fought back the tears of images with the strength of knowing that he was worthy of the gods.

Over the next couple of weeks, as Pazou and Ori were resting and healing, Zoonee delivered messages and instructions to the young men.

"Ori wants to question the man," she said to them. So, the three of them took the blonde-haired man to the shelter to see Ori. Ori had managed to sit up and so had Pazou. Pazou and Ori were just finishing a prayer to Asclepius, the god of healing, as the young men entered with their prisoner. The teenagers sat the man down in front of them to speak.

Ori, glaring at the man who shot him,

"I need to know what Gorlev plans to do next. If you tell me, I will escort you back through the portal; you have my word," Ori said, earnestly, awaiting the man's response.

"How do I know I can trust you?" The man questioned.

"Gorlev left you. We can escort you back to Germany. It seems to me that you have no choice. It would seem that Gorlev does not value your service or sacrifice for his purpose," Ori asserted. "It seems that you should ask yourself whether or not you can trust your leader."

The man looked down at the ground for a few moments. He seemed to realize that Ori might be right, not to mention that they had been very kind to him: feeding him, giving him water, and allowing him to relieve himself.

"I ...," he hesitated, "I have only heard whispers," he responded, reluctantly.

"What did those whispers say?" Ori asked, amiably.

"Gorlev seeks another Ring Bearer...," he paused to remember, "Something like prophecy, somewhere in Asia," he continued. Ori's eyes widened at this news, and he immediately knew Gorlev's next maneuver.

Ori, after a few moments of silence,

"Okay, thank you for your cooperation. When I am strong enough, I will take you home," Ori stated, promising the man with his eyes. The man didn't reply; he only gazed at Ori. *How could a man be so kind to me after I had shot him?* The nameless soldier thought to himself. The boys took the man back to the tree, but not before giving him something to eat and to drink.

133

Ori looked at Pazou from across the shelter.

"We have to get to him or to *her* first," Pazou said, reading Ori's mind. Ori nodded in agreement. They knew that Gorlev was searching for the Ring Bearer of the Silver Ring of Prophecy and his Guardian. They also knew that they would have to teleport to Asia to find them first. They didn't have long to heal their wounds.

That night, as Jimmy was standing guard, watching their prisoner, he began to think about his mother and father again. He began to miss them. He knew that time was standing still for them, but he wondered what would happen if he were to die during this vital adventure. *Would they miss him? Would they know that he was gone?* He thought to himself. These were questions that haunted him, questions that he felt he had to suppress.

He heard footsteps behind him. As he turned, he saw Ryan, Zoonee, and Parelo headed toward him, cheerfully. They had been discussing the battle, re-enacting it for each other. They were excited and displayed a new confidence in themselves and in one another. They had become a dedicated, potent team.

It made him feel better to know that he was not alone in this mission. He had proven friends who would protect

134

and support him. There was no longer any friction between him and Parelo. He watched as Parelo and Ryan sat down together across from the campfire, laughing and exchanging stories.

Zoonee quietly sat down beside him on the other side. Jimmy poked at the fire with a stick and smiled on the inside at what was taking place between her and himself. He turned to see her drawing in the dirt again. As he looked down at her drawing, he saw a heart with his and her initials written within it. He raised his head to meet her eyes staring back at his. This time, he took her hand.

Chapter Nine
The First Break

Several days later, Jimmy decided to go speak to Ori about his parents. He had become homesick, and he didn't know how to cope with his feelings. They had rebuilt four new shelters after Gorlev had burnt down all of them. Jimmy slowly opened the door to Ori's shelter to see if he was awake or not.

Ori was awake, but he was lying down. He hadn't quite healed from his wound, and he also realized that he might not ever have the range of motion and strength in his left arm again. Ori was contemplating his condition and the near future as Jimmy walked in and stood above him.

"Good morning, Ori," he said. "How are you feeling?"

"Old," Ori replied, "but better each day. How are you?" Jimmy looked to his right and then down, wondering if he should bother him with his concerns. He didn't want to seem insensitive, and he knew Ori was in worse shape.

"It's...," he hesitated, not wanting Ori to think that he was weak, "just that I miss my parents," he finally admitted. Ori smiled, understanding Jimmy's feelings and circumstances.

"I understand, Jimmy," he stated. "There's nothing wrong with *you* or the *way* you feel. As a matter of fact, I think we could all use a reprieve before we begin the next phase of our mission. I will speak to Pazou and the others, and see how they feel about going home to rest for a while. What do you think?" he asked.

Jimmy, lifting his head in relief,

"I think that is a great idea," he said, beaming at Ori.

"Great, then we will plan to leave tomorrow morning." With that, Jimmy felt better about himself, and he was anxious to see his parents and go back home for a break. He lightly squeezed Ori's right hand while peering into his comforting azure eyes. He couldn't wait to share the news with Ryan.

Jimmy went back into his shelter as Ryan was stretching. Ryan saw Jimmy come in and grinned at him.

"I gotta stretch before I train, so I won't pull a muscle," he said, bending to the right and then to the left. Jimmy grinned at him, and went over quickly to his pallet to sit down, so he could tell him the good news.

"What muscle?" he asked, making fun of him. "Hey, man, sit down. I got something to tell you. I think you are going to like it." Ryan sat down on his pallet to listen to Jimmy.

"Okay, so, Ori said that he thinks we all need a little break, and I think he also needs time to heal, you know? So, he thinks we should all go home to rest for a while before we start again," he explained, beaming.

"Yeah!" Ryan exclaimed, holding up both his arms in a V shape. "That's *awesome*, dude. When are we going? I can't wait to see my mom," he added, excited.

"Ori said that we could leave tomorrow morning, but he wants to speak to the others first." As Jimmy heard himself say the others, he realized that he would have to part ways with Zoonee. He began to fill a little emptiness inside his stomach. He wanted to see his parents, but he didn't want to leave her. Ryan, observing his lack of enthusiasm, knew what was wrong.

"Hey, man, it's not forever. It's just for a little while. Go talk to her. I'm sure she will understand. Besides, this will give her a chance to see her grandparents and cousins," he added, Jimmy looked up into his green eyes and knew he was right.

"Yeah, you're right, man," he admitted, feeling better about his decision. "She will understand and will be happy that she has an opportunity to see her family." Jimmy sat there with Ryan, discussing what they were going to do once they got back home.

Ori, making it to his feet, headed over to Pazou and Zoonee's shelter. It had been weeks, but Ori still had excruciating pain in his shoulder. He couldn't spin his staff with his left arm, which would ultimately limit his ability to block bullets—and perhaps, even balls of fire.

He slowly moved back the opening to their shelter and could see that Zoonee was attending to Pazou's bandages. Zoonee glanced toward him.

"Oh, I will come back later," Ori said, trying to give Zoonee time to aid Pazou.

"It's okay, my friend," said Pazou. "We are just about finished," he added, trying to sit up so he could see Ori. Ori stepped inside as Zoonee placed the last bandage on his left arm.

"Good morning friends," Ori began. "I have some important news that I want to share with you." Zoonee sat down beside Pazou and gave Ori her undivided attention.

"I think we need a break before we start the next phase of our mission. I think we should all go home for a while. This way we can all rest and visit family and friends. What do you two think?" he added, desiring to hear their opinion. Zoonee smiled at Ori and then at Pazou. Pazou turned to see her happy disposition. He smiled hard and turned back to face Ori.

"I think that would be just fine," he stated, amicably. "We could all use a change of scenery and a good rest with family and friends."

Ori, grinning, "Is tomorrow morning alright?"

"Yes!" replied Zoonee, not waiting for Pazou to respond. Pazou laughed loudly at this.

"I think we have our answer, my friend," he said. With that, Ori bowed to them both and headed to Parelo's shelter. He met Parelo halfway, as he was about to head into Jimmy and Ryan's shelter to wake them.

"Hey, Parelo," he began. "May I have a moment of your time," he asked, politely. Parelo stopped before entering the shelter and turned to face Ori with an apprehensive demeanor. Ori, noticing, decided to put him at ease.

"Oh, it's alright. It's a good thing," he assured him.

Parelo, relieved, smiled and stood still, awaiting his message.

"We think that it is time for us to go home to rest and to spend some time with our families and friends. What do you think about that?" he asked, expecting a jubilant response. Parelo lowered his head. Ori, a little dumbfounded by his reaction to his news, wrinkled his forehead, but gave Parelo ample time to explain his unusual response.

"It sounds good to all of you, but I have no family left," he explained, lowering his eyes again. "You all are my only family," he said, somberly. Ori immediately understood and came over to him, placing his good arm on Parelo's right shoulder.

"I didn't realize...," he began, "but then you are like me and Pazou. This is our family, too—and you are certainly a part of it. You can come home with me. And, perhaps, Ryan and Jimmy can introduce you to their parents as a friend," he added. This cheered Parelo up; and, without warning, he hugged Ori tightly around his waist, tears falling from both his brown cheeks. Ori hugged him as snuggly as he could, though the pain in his shoulder was intense.

Ori, almost crying himself, spoke:

"It will be okay, Parelo. You will *never* have to worry about not having a family to care for you," he promised. After a few moments, Parelo let go and looked up into Ori's bright blue, friendly eyes.

"Thank you," he replied. That was all he said, and then he let go of Ori just in time to meet the boys coming out of their shelter, overhearing most of what was spoken by them. Ryan came up to Parelo and hugged him heavily.

"You will always have a home with me. Jimmy's my brother, and you are my other brother," he said, affectionately. "You will never be alone, man. I can talk my mother into anything. You can stay with me, and we will have some fun. We will watch movies, listen to music, spend the night at Jimmy's, and play my Z-box III," he expounded. "It will be the bomb-diggity!" At that, Jimmy, who was standing behind Parelo, holding on to one of his shoulders, laughed loudly, causing Zoonee and Pazou to come out of their shelter.

Ori, seeing Pazou and Zoonee, turned toward them.

"I was just giving Parelo the good news," he said. "Parelo is going back home with us for now." Pazou nodded and Zoonee smiled at Parelo, who stood between Ori and Ryan. He was filled with joy, and he felt accepted. He no longer felt alone.

After a few minutes, Ori reminded everyone that they needed to send their captive home before they could leave. They had decided to build him a small hut, but they had to keep him tied up to a post in the middle of it because they still didn't trust him. Ori and Pazou went into his hut and untied him, so he could eat and drink. They kept an eye on him while this was taking place.

When he was finished eating, Ori and Pazou took him to the portal.

"Where are you taking me, now?" he asked, apprehensively. Pazou turned to him, but he only said one word:

"Home." The man put his head down.

"Thank you. I will never forget the mercy you have shown me." Ori and Pazou looked at each other and then to the man. Ori recited the words, and they were gone.

While Pazou and Ori were on their way to Germany to take back their prisoner, Jimmy decided to speak to Zoonee about going home and to say goodbye to her. She was in her hut, which she shared with Pazou, getting ready to head back to Antarctica. Jimmy slowly pulled back the opening to the shelter.

"Hey, Zoonee, can I talk to you for second?" he asked. Zoonee folded an article of clothing and turned to him, half-smiling.

"Hey, yeah, of course," she said, knowing the reason and message that would follow. He sat down on his knees beside her.

"I want to see my parents, but I'm...," he paused and looked down.

"I know, me, too. But, this is not over. Our work is not done, and we will be back together soon," she smiled, placing her left hand on his and looking into his face until his eyes moved upward to meet hers. Jimmy nodded and leaned in for a hug. They held each other for a few moments before letting go. Zoonee felt a tear trickle down her cheek and onto Jimmy's shoulder. They released each other and Jimmy looked into her small, dark eyes.

"I'll be back for you," he promised. At that, Zoonee sniffed and quickly nodded.

"I know," she assured him. Jimmy got to his feet, turning one more time, and then left the shelter.

Later that evening, Ori and Pazou returned, and they all gathered by the campfire to fellowship. They kept the conversations light, going around the circle, telling each other what they were going to do once they were home. Zoonee went first.

"I'm going to see my grandmother and cousins," she said, looking around the circle at the others. Jimmy went next.

"I'm going to see my parents," he said, glancing at Zoonee. Then it was Ryan's turn.

"I'm going to visit with my mom and watch *Star Tales V* with Parelo," he grinned. Everyone erupted in simultaneous laughter at his candid response.

After visiting for a while, Ori and Pazou praised them for their effort, diligence, and dedication to their cause. They said their goodbyes and headed toward their shelters for the night.

The next morning, they gathered in front of the portal. Pazou and Zoonee went first.

"Goodbye, my friends. We will see you soon," he said, as Zoonee turned to wave to Jimmy and the others. Pazou repeated the words, and they were gone. Ori turned to have another look at the place where he and his father had trained, knowing that he would never see it again. Somehow, the young men knew what he was thinking, but they didn't want to interrupt his moment of remembrance. Ori smiled at them, turned to face the invisible portal, and spoke the words.

Chapter Ten
The Next Project

They all arrived seconds later in Ori's rustic cabin. Ori took in the smell of the stew that he had been cooking before meeting the boys. He instructed Jimmy and Ryan to leave their gifts with him until the time had come for them to rejoin the team. The Azure Ring, as if it knew what was happening, unwound itself from Jimmy's ring finger, and Jimmy placed it into Ori's open palm. Likewise, Ryan handed Ori his staff and his cane, while Parelo looked on sullenly, knowing that he had lost his gift to the enemy.

Ryan, noticed Parelo's reaction.

"It'll be okay, man. We'll get it back," he comforted. "I will come get you Monday afternoon and introduce you to my mom. I'll tell her that you are a foreign exchange student, and you have come to visit your *Uncle* Ori. But, you can't go to the same school, obviously. She'll buy it; don't worry," he said, patting him on the shoulder. "I don't want you to have to stay the entire time with Ori," he said, causing Parelo and Ori to grin.

Parelo nodded and hugged Ryan. They shook hands with Ori, and the boys headed for the door. Before they opened the cabin door, Ori had one last message:

"Be careful my young friends. If you need me, I will be here, mending my wounds. When I am ready to fight again, I will come for you. In the meantime, enjoy being with your family and friends," he said, to which the boys nodded in agreement.

As soon as their feet hit the ground they were running through the clearing and to the opening in the cave. They slowed down as they crawled through the cave to the end of the passageway. They hopped down from the nook and made their way to the stairs. Once they were out of the cave, they paused to catch their breath.

They tracked through the thick vegetation until they hit the pavement. When they made it to the road, Ryan and Jimmy put their arms in the air, looking up at the moon. Nothing had changed, and it even took them less time to run from Ori's home through the cavern. Because they were ahead of schedule, they thanked the gods and decided to walk the rest of the way back to Ryan's house. When they arrived at Ryan's home, the boys climbed back into Ryan's bedroom window and went fast to sleep.

The next morning Jimmy woke up on Ryan's Star Tale's bean bag to the voice of his father who was directly above him.

"Hey, wake up, Jim," his father said, grinning. "It's almost noon, and we need to head back home for lunch, and I don't want to miss the game." Jimmy yawned and stretched out his arms. He could hear Ryan waking over to his right on his bed that was decked out in Star Tale's sheets. Normally, Jimmy would have grumbled and asked to stay longer, but not today.

Jimmy grinned.

"Okay, Dad. Let's do it." Jimmy's father was speechless and stunned by his reply. He was certain Jimmy would try to negotiate for more time and make him come back later that day to get him. He observed that Jimmy and Ryan were still wearing their shoes, and they were very dirty. He decided not to say anything since Jimmy was being cooperative.

After Jimmy reached his feet, still looking cheerful, he hugged his father. His father, naturally, was a little suspicious, but the unexpected display of affection actually made him feel better about his relationship with his son. He hugged Jimmy back, and they said goodbye to Ryan and his mother.

On the way home, Jimmy and his father were both in a good mood. They discussed watching the Kansas Eagles play football.

"So, you want to watch the Kansas Eagles game with me?" his father asked, somewhat doubtful. The Kansas Eagles was his father's favorite FAL or Football Alliance League team, and he was a loyal fan, too, though he had never seen a live game. He said seeing them play was on his bucket list, though Jimmy had never understood the metaphor.

Usually, Jimmy's answer would have been, "Nah, I have got to do homework," or another excuse to get out of having to watch the game with his father. He wasn't much of a sport's fan and considered most jocks to be egotistical, alpha males at best. The only sport that he had ever played was ping pong, but he wasn't really sure that it qualified as a real sport. He was also on the chess team at school, but he wasn't sure about that one either. What he did know, however, was that they were not popular in Newford. But, today, he decided to give it a shot, not because of sports, but because of his father.

"Yeah, that sounds cool," he said. He glanced over to see his father smile to himself while trying to concentrate on the road.

"Maybe today, after the game," he began, "we could even work on some old computers in the garage and drink some sweet, ice tea. Jimmy's father loved tinkering with old computers on a Sunday afternoon. "I'll show you a few things," he added. Again, normally, Jimmy passed on such activities. He realized that he wanted to spend time with his father now and to allow him to teach him his trade.

Maybe I was too busy for him, not the other way around, he thought to himself.

"Sure," he responded. "I'd like to learn more about computers...You know, the circuits, wires, and stuff." His father beamed at him for a second and then turned back to the right to the side road that led to their home.

Once home, Jimmy walked in, turned right, and could see that his mother had already prepared the meal for the day: pizza from Little Shelby's. He walked quickly to the kitchen, grabbed a plate from the cabinet and almost ran to the table.

"Whoa, slow down, there, Son," his father said with a chuckle. "You act like you haven't had pizza in years." Jimmy didn't comment. Instead, he snatched four pizzas of thin crust Pepperoni and began to decimate them.

"Man, this is so good," he said, devouring the first two pieces. His father grabbed a plate from the cabinet and slowly lifted two pieces from the blue and white box. He thought Jimmy's actions were peculiar, but then he remembered that his son was still a teenage boy.

As they were eating, his mother came in through the front door. She had been grocery shopping for the upcoming week. Jimmy scarfed down his third piece and lifted his head to greet her.

"Hey, Mom," he said, going over to help her with the grocery bags. He helped her put up the groceries, which he had never done before, and then he reached around to hug her.

"Love ya, Mom," he said, and he went to his bedroom to get clothes, so he could shower. His mother called after him.

"Love you, too," she replied, glancing over at his father. His father shrugged, shook his head, and continued eating.

After finishing his shower, Jimmy met his father in the living room to watch the New York Lasers play the Kansas Eagles. He set down in one of their brown, leather recliners, facing their flat screen television, and his father handed him a grape soda. Jimmy observed how happy his father was and knew it was because he had chosen to spend the day with him.

As they watched the game, Jimmy's mind began to wonder. He began to wonder what Zoonee was doing and if she was safe from harm. He wished that she was there with him, but he also knew that was an impossibility given their different circumstances. He realized that this was the first time in months that he hadn't awoke to find her sitting around the campfire, waiting for him to come to visit with her. He also wondered what Ryan was doing and how he was adjusting to being home again after being absent for so long.

"Go! Go! Go!" his dad cheered, as the Eagles tight end ran into the end zone for a touchdown. Jimmy's thoughts were interrupted by his father's elation, so he decided to join in with some applause.

That afternoon, Jimmy ate the last of the pizzas, and then he joined him out in the garage to tinker with some old computers that needed maintenance. They worked on an older unit that had a broken PS/8 port. They had to order the part from a company that no longer made the unit, but who still carried some of the parts.

His father had Jimmy pick up another unit that had been sitting around for a while. He showed Jimmy how to upgrade the unit's RAM and explained how to order the correct memory modules if he ever had to do it himself. Jimmy didn't think the work was fascinating, but he was intrigued by the fact that his father did.

Secretly, Jimmy knew his father wanted him to follow in his footsteps, but he also knew that his father wanted him to go beyond what he had accomplished. He had high expectations for Jimmy, which is why he pushed him so hard in school and around the house. Naturally, Jimmy had the propensity to rebel, as with all teenagers, but somehow Jimmy could tell that his recent experiences had modified his previous inclinations.

"Okay, you just snap the memory down into the PCI slot, and...*voila*! This should make the unit process a little faster and the programs should run more smoothly," he explained to Jimmy.

That night, as Jimmy was lying in his bed, he began to think about the day and himself. He looked inward-- something he rarely even considered doing--and discovered a few important characteristics and qualities that he had developed during his time in an obvious alternate reality. What he hadn't realized, until that day with his father, was how that reality had shaped his own. He realized that he had become more mature over the past few months, but he had no other choice. He also learned how to make sacrifices for others and how significant it was to do so. Finally, he had learned to be dedicated to a cause that was more about others than it was about himself. He strongly desired to divulge his secret to his parents, but he knew that he could not—for their sake.

Jimmy enjoyed spending the day working with his father and learning how to repair computers. He was even looking forward to the next Sunday afternoon with his father. He was also looking forward to seeing Ryan and discussing his latest revelations.

It was Monday afternoon, and Jimmy was riding home with his mother, as he always did because his father had to stay until 4:30. He considered his day and how surreal it was to be back in the classroom among the other teenagers. He and Ryan sat at the same table in the lunchroom, as they always had, and discussed their first days back at Newford. They both agreed that it was great, but it was also different. They both admitted that there were times when they felt that they didn't belong back in Newford, but they didn't take these feelings to heart. They assumed that they would adjust to being back home, just as they had acclimated to being away from it.

While on lunch break, they had met privately on some bleachers beside the football field. They decided to concoct a plan, so they could get together on a school night, which was usually taboo. Their ploy was to say that they had a science project to complete, and it would require spending a few days a week with each other for the next few months. They knew that their parents might check it out, but they couldn't come up with anything else.

Jimmy decided to ask his mom while his dad was away. His mom was more likely to consent to a request of this sort, especially since it had something to do with school.

"Hey, Mom, I need to go to Ryan's house a few days a week to work on a science project. Can you take me there, today?" he asked, slightly nervous, but not as nervous as he would have been if he had asked his father the same question. His mother pondered his query for a second, and then answered.

"Yes, I guess, but what is the science project? You know I will have to explain it to your father. And, how long will you need to be there each afternoon? You know how exhausted your father and I are when we first get home from work." Yes, Jimmy knew, so he had to think fast. He and Ryan hadn't really discussed the specifics.

"It's for the Science Fair," he quickly answered. "We are trying to prove the theoretical existence of an alternate reality." His mother studied his answer, but she ultimately decided that it sounded legitimate.

"Okay, that sounds really interesting. I want to see it when you have finished it," she added, excited. *Crap!* Jimmy thought to himself.

"Cool, no problem," he muttered. He went to his bedroom to text Ryan. He hated lying to his parents, but he rationalized that it was an ongoing alternate reality project that would negatively affect the entire human population. He knew, however, that they would eventually find out, and he had to tell Ryan immediately.

To: Ryan;

Me: "Hey, we need to talk...I told my mom we were doing a science project on alternate reality."

Ryan: "What the hell? You couldn't think of something easier, like finding the insulating temperatures of different fabrics or something?"

Me: "I panicked, okay, gimme a break!"

Ryan: "Fine. I'll figure out something. Hang on, my mom is callin' me..."

Me: "OK."

Ryan: "Well, now my mom knows. It only took your mother about 10 milliseconds to ask my mother about our little science project. You do realize that we can't prove this, right? Well, we can, but we would have to use your ring or my staff."

Me: "It's theoretical. Besides, you're the one that is big on Star Tales. Can't you come up with something?"

Ryan: "Hey, you saw the movie, too, okay. Be nice. Yeah, probably. I just need some time think, jerk."

Me: "OK. I'll be over in a little while—Geek."

Ryan: "Alright, man lol."

After his conversation with Ryan, Jimmy realized that he had matured some, but he was still a teenage boy. He chuckled to himself, and then grabbed his backpack. He heard his mother open the door and the keys rattled. He knew it was time to go, and he couldn't wait to see Ori and Parelo.

When Jimmy arrived at Ryan's, he got out of his mom's 2018, silver Cadillac and bumped fists with him. His mother got out briefly to speak to Ms. Trigee. The boys ran inside to prepare for their project. Ryan found an old rocket, and he thought he might tell his mom that they needed to go down the road to the wooded area to shoot it because the ground was more elevated, which they would use to somehow support their hypothesis.

After convincing his mother of the scientific merit involved in launching a small rocket into the air, his mother agreed to let them go. They knew that they didn't have much time, so they ran to the wooded area and moved cautiously, but quickly, through the cave.

When they made it to the cabin, they caught their breath, and Parelo, seeing them, opened the door.

"Hi," he said congenially. "Come inside. Ori and I just finished eating some stew." The boys remembered the first time they had entered the cabin and snickered to each other about the smell of the stew.

Ori, getting up from his rocking chair,

"Welcome, young men. How was your weekend?" he asked jovially. The boys hugged Parelo and Ori before answering his question.

"Awesome—but a little weird, too," Ryan admitted. "It was weird not having to wear the same underwear each day." Everyone laughed at this, though Ori had showed them how to wash and how to dry their clothes. Jimmy echoed Ryan's answer.

"It is weird...," he began, "But not simply because of the changes we had to make while we were there. It's different because we are different. We have changed. What we value and our opinions have changed. But, we are still teens in this world," he ended his explanation, which Ori, Parelo, and Ryan perceived as wise. "What I used to think was boring, now, I think it's interesting and important," he continued, while the others listened patiently. They seemed to grasp the crux of his statement, and Ori understood them all too well. He had been teleporting back and forth since he was Jimmy's age.

"I believe we all understand, Jimmy," Ori responded, maintaining eye contact with him. "Our choices change us, and their reasons determine our reality." With that, the boys and Ori went outside to talk. Ori gave Jimmy his ring and Ryan his staff to practice. Parelo looked on with Ori.

Jimmy produced a rainbow of water in the clearing, and Ryan created a vortex of leaves, swirling up into the air like a DNA strand. Then, Ryan had an idea: He took the rocket out of his backpack, and he let Parelo light the fuse.

Poof! The small rocket launched high into the air. Parelo had never lit the fuse of a rocket before, not even on the Fourth of July, so this was a thrilling moment for him. Ryan explained to him that the real rockets, built by engineers, used the same, basic concepts to send a huge one millions of miles into space.

The boys visited with Parelo and Ori for a couple of hours. Ryan looked down at his phone.

"Well, it's time to go," he said, looking at Jimmy. "We will be back tomorrow," he told Parelo. "This weekend you can stay the night at my house." Parelo grinned and fist bumped Ryan and Jimmy, and the teens waved goodbye to Ori.

Chapter Eleven
The Bad Idea

Their first weekend had finally come, and the boys were ready to spend the night together and introduce Parelo to Ryan's mother. Jimmy awoke, but he didn't lay in bed as usual, staring up at his poster of May Sting. He had another girl on his mind, so he leaped out of bed and headed for the bathroom to shower.

He had forgotten what it was like to have certain luxuries, like bathrooms and showers. He appreciated them more now than ever. As he changed into his clothes and packed his bag for Ryan's, he wondered how he had accomplished so much: how he was able to give up so much and how he was able to face life and death situations at every turn. He confessed to himself that he didn't know, but he was proud that he was able to rise to the occasion. He hoped that he would be brave enough and strong enough to do it again. He wasn't sure when Ori would be ready to travel or to battle, but he had packed a special bag for the trip this time.

He walked down the hallway from his bedroom to the kitchen. His father and mother were doing what they had always done on the weekends. His father was the first one to notice him this time.

"Good morning, Jim," he said, looking up from his paper. Jimmy glanced at his mother who was looking directly at him with a warm smile. She was proud of Jimmy for spending time with his father because she enjoyed seeing them bonding.

"So, what do you guys have planned for tomorrow," she asked them. Jimmy's father looked up at her.

"Well," he began, glancing in Jimmy's direction, "We will probably watch the Eagles play the Las Vegas Sharks," he stated, as he winked at Jimmy.

"Right," he replied, and he headed to the kitchen for some breakfast.

His father dropped him off at Ryan's house and then headed back. Ryan, as usual, was sitting on his porch with a big smile on his face. Before Jimmy could make it there, Ryan jumped off the third step and took off toward him.

"Hey, come on!" he urged. "Let's go get Parelo. I've already discussed it with mom." Jimmy tossed his bag of clothes on the porch and sprinted to catch up with Ryan.

When they arrived at the clearing, they saw Parelo and Ori standing outside having a conversation. They slowed up as the two of them turned to meet them. Neither Ori, nor Parelo, was smiling. Something was wrong.

Ori faced them both.

"We have a serious problem," he said, in a matter of fact tone of voice. The boys could sense the urgency of the situation. Before Ori could explain, his cabin door opened and out walked Zoonee. They noticed that Pazou was not with her.

"What's happened?" asked Jimmy, somewhat frantically. "Is Zoonee or Pazou hurt?" Ori motioned for Zoonee to come join them. She walked slowly over to meet them. The closer she came, the easier it was for them to make out her appearance. She had been weeping, so much so that the tears had dried and caused streaks down her cheeks.

Jimmy walked over to hug her.

"What is it? What happened?" he pleaded for her to answer him.

"Pazou...," she hesitated, "has been captured by Gorlev and his men," she answered, as her voice

165

cracked. "Gorlev found us in Antarctica. He demanded that I give him the ring or else. Pazou refused to allow it, so we fought." She lifted up her shirt so that they could all see where she had been burnt by Gorlev. "I couldn't keep them from taking him. They shot him in the leg, and Gorlev burned him again. I don't know if he is alive or dead. Pazou told me to run to the portal, so I did. I said the words of a Ring Bearer, and now I am here. I failed to protect him," she said, somberly.

Everyone stayed quiet for several minutes, and then Jimmy spoke.

"You did what you had to do. You can't give him your ring, and we will get Pazou back," he said, determined and angry. Ryan came closer to Zoonee and Jimmy.

"Yeah, we'll get him back, and we'll give this monster what he has comin' to him," Ryan promised.

"Let's go inside and finish this conversation," Ori suggested. "We will do everything in our power to free Pazou, Zoonee."

Once inside, Zoonee explained to them what happened with more detail.

"Gorlev caught us both off guard. We thought he was looking for the Ring Bearer of Prophecy. Pazou was feeling better, and he was beginning to twirl his staff with both arms, though the pain still lingered. I went to visit my grandma and cousins for a few days, and then I came back to check on him," she took a deep breath. "When I got there, Gorlev and his men had him. I froze their bullets and three of the men. I even created an ice container around Pazou, so the men could not touch him. But, Gorlev was too strong, and the dark man was too powerful. He made me bow in submission, and Gorlev melted the container around Pazou. While I was on my knees, crying, Pazou was able to free himself long enough to throw his staff with one good arm and hit the dark man in the head, causing him to lose his concentration and control over me. Pazou instructed me to run for the portal and not to look back. But, I did look back, and I saw them shoot him in the leg, and...," she hesitated, "I saw Gorlev hit him in the chest with a flaming ball of fire." She ended her account, and she put her head down and began to weep again.

Jimmy, vehemently, "He must be *stopped*! This has to *end*!" he repeated for Ori, who could only nod in agreement.

"I know where he is: He is in Germany. I can focus on finding Pazou, and then we can go rescue him. But, that must be our only objective, for now," he said, making sure that everyone understood him.

"Let's get him, now!" Parelo, declared, who had been sitting quietly by himself until now. Ori and the boys turned to see that he, too, was very angry and eager to exact vengeance.

Ori, calmly, to all of them,

"We must be patient. I need a day to work out a plan of action. If he is at the barn where we freed our captive, then we can use it to our advantage. But, you all must remember: Gorlev will know that we are coming to save Pazou. Rushing into this would be foolish, and that could cause us to lose someone else. We must outsmart him," he insisted.

As Ori finished speaking, the boys and Zoonee knew he was right. An unplanned attack could result in another capture or worse. They had to accept the fact that they were fighting, not just for Pazou, but for everyone else as well.

Later that evening, the boys decided that it would be best not to take Parelo back with them. They had to rest, get prepared, and say their goodbyes to their parents. They didn't know how long they would be away this time. They were even uncertain about whether or not they would ever return.

Jimmy helped Ryan pack up his clothes and other necessities that they didn't have the first time. Jimmy leaned back on Ryan's Star Tale's bean bag, thinking about the situation and the future. He was ready for vindication, but he also knew the risks that were involved and worried about Zoonee's safety, along with Ryan's. He knew he was a part of an unfathomable adventure, but he wondered if it was worth the costs. *He and Ryan were only teenagers; they had their whole lives to live*, he thought to himself. He quickly placed his mind on Zoonee and Pazou, trying not to lose his perspective. He got up abruptly and went over to Ryan's bedroom window, leaning over with his forearm, catching his weight on the metal frame. He was looking out at nothing, but thinking about everything.

Ryan paused his game to glance over at him. He, too, was trying to distract himself, but was having no luck.

"Was this a mistake, Ryan?" he asked, still peering out of the window pane at nothing. Ryan contemplated his question for several minutes. Jimmy turned his head back to him, squinting, sensing that Ryan was facing the same mental turmoil.

Finally, Ryan spoke:

"No, I don't believe that...I refuse to believe that this isn't our destiny," he said, sincerely, lifting his head to face Jimmy's questioning eyes. "Yes, it is very, very hard. But, life is hard. Sometimes you have to make tough choices— 'and stand by those choices.'" Jimmy's eyes grew large, as Ryan quoted Pazou's words to him after Parelo had left.

"Exactly!" Jimmy concurred. He had an idea. "We are going to go get Pazou—tonight!" Ryan looked at Jimmy, flabbergasted at first, but he realized that it might work. He remembered that his plan worked, so he knew there was a chance.

"They will never see it coming," he continued. "They will be expecting all of us, not two of us. We will sneak in, grab Pazou, undetected, and teleport back home before the sun comes up," he explained.

"Okay, you went along with my crazy rescue scheme, so I'm going to help you with yours," he answered, getting to his feet to lock hands with Jimmy. "Let's go get our Pazou back, dammit!" Jimmy smiled, they grabbed their bags, and hopped out Ryan's bedroom window for the road.

When they reached the clearing, they saw a shadow move inside the cabin. As they crept closer, trying to sneak in and to the portal without being noticed, Zoonee opened the door.

"What are you two doing here?" she asked. "You guys aren't supposed to come here until tomorrow." Jimmy glanced at Ryan and then they both looked at Zoonee.

"Oh my *gods*, really?" she replied, guessing their intentions. "There is no way, this time," she said, holding up her hands to emphasize her point. "Gorlev is expecting us. He will have men everywhere." Jimmy and Ryan didn't say a word. They just kept glancing at each other and then to Zoonee.

The boys could feel Zoonee's irritated glower as she tried to convince them not to go. Then, her face suddenly changed; her eyes began to glow, along with her body. The boys slowly backed down the cabin steps to brace themselves for her wrath.

"I'm going, too. Don't ever, ever try to leave me out rescuing someone close to me again. Do you understand?" she asked, rhetorically. The boys answered gently and nearly in unison:

"Yep, sorry, Zoonee; won't happen again," they said, apologetically. With that Zoonee calmed herself and the glowing dissipated almost as quickly as it had appeared. The boys had no choice, but to agree with her and to allow her to go with them.

They snuck inside the cabin. Parelo and Ori were sleeping soundly in the other room. Ori had an old, wooden chest where he kept their weapons. Jimmy carefully lifted the lid on the chest, just enough to grab his ring, Ryan's staff, and cane for light. They moved over to the hearth.

Zoonee whispered the ancient words:

"In the name of the gods, give us Ring Bearers passage."

Chapter Twelve
The Brave Soldier

It was dusk in Germany as they stood under the old tree with the ancient posts slightly behind them. They ducked down because they knew that Gorlev's men could clearly see them from the top of the hill on which the large white house stood. They decided to crawl to the edge of the hill, where they could hide behind some large rocks and bushes.

Everything was quiet. As far as they could tell, there were only two lights on in the house, one upstairs and one downstairs. They decided to go over their plan.

"Okay," Jimmy began. "Pazou is probably being held in the red barn like Parelo." He checked to see if Zoonee and Ryan were listening to him. They both nodded their heads in agreement. "So, let's try to do what we did before, alright? That way, if there are men in the barn, then we have the element of surprise on our side again," he explained.

"But, do you think the *same* plan will work?" he questioned. Zoonee looked over at Jimmy for second, echoing Ryan's concerns with her penetrating eyes.

"This seems too easy," Zoonee suggested. "Gorlev is a military leader, Jimmy. He's not going to fall for the same thing."

"It will work because it is the same thing," he assured them. "Gorlev won't be ready for the same rescue attempt."

"If you say so, man, but I don't like this. I'm with Zoonee," Ryan admitted. Jimmy mulled over their advice for a second before making a decision.

"Okay, I'll go alone. If it is a trap, then they will only get me. But, you two must promise me that you will go back to get Ori and Parelo," he retorted. Ryan and Zoonee both agreed.

"Here, take my cane for light," Ryan said, handing Jimmy his foot-long cane.

"Thanks, man, I'll need it for sure," he admitted.

"Be careful," Zoonee warned.

"I will," he assured her.

Jimmy moved quietly, but swiftly, to the red barn. He didn't have a ladder this time, so he had to sneak in from the front, which he knew was risky. He lifted the wooden beam which held the door shut and opened the door. It was dark, quiet, but he could hear chains moving to his right. He was certain that it was Pazou. He used Ryan's cane to light up the barn so he could see clearly.

It was Pazou, and he looked dreadful. Jimmy scanned his body to evaluate whether or not he would be able to walk or if he would have to get Zoonee and Ryan to help him carry Pazou out and to the portal. His leg had been bandaged, his chest looked scarred by fire, and Pazou's head was sweating.

He flashed the light into Pazou's face, but what he saw was not pleasant. Pazou's eyes displayed a look of horror, one that frightened Jimmy more than staring down Gorlev himself. Pazou's voice was muffled by thick strips of duct tape over his mouth. He could tell that Pazou was in unbearable pain. Jimmy stood on one knee in terror as he had never seen someone so brave look so devastated by his circumstances. He decided to go get Zoonee and Ryan to help free him.

Just as he was about to go out the entrance of the barn, someone hit him hard over the head: He was out...

When he came to, Jimmy found himself on some hay, and the back of his head was throbbing from the hard blow it took from the end of a rifle. He sat upright and his eyesight was a little blurry. He looked straight ahead and could see that he was in a cell of some kind. He saw another cell across from him and a chair on the outside of it up against the wall. Someone was in the cell: It was Pazou. They had moved him from the barn to a cell. Jimmy was about to call out to him, but he could hear footsteps coming from nearby. It sounded like two people were coming toward him and Pazou. Then they stopped in between his cell and Pazou's. It was Gorlev and the dark man with the Ring of Dominion.

"Welcome, my friend," he began, sitting down in the chair with the back of it facing Jimmy. "How do you like your new home," he asked, sarcastically. The dark man grinned at Jimmy.

Jimmy didn't answer.

Gorlev looked up, left, and then right. "This basement was used to hold POW's back during World War II," he said, nostalgically. "If you get bored, you could nose through the hay. You might find some bones," he said with a wicked smirk. His memory was interrupted by coughs that came from Pazou's cell. "Or, you could simply wait until your friend dies, and then you can have his

176

bones," he replied. Jimmy looked up at him, but refused to speak. "Such a young, brave boy. It would be a shame to waste such talent. You could join me, you know. Then you wouldn't have to worry about dying an egregious death," he grinned. "I'll let you *think* on it." He got up and moved the chair back against the rock wall, and he and the dark man left snickering.

Jimmy looked down at his finger and saw that his ring had been removed. There was a little cut around his ring finger where they had pried it loose. He was helpless, in a cell with no food, some water in a small bucket, and a lots of hay. He got to his feet and went over to the bars of his cell to see about Pazou. He could hear him breathing heavily and knew he needed medical attention immediately.

"Pazou, Pazou," he called out, raising his voice a little each time. "Can you hear me? It's Jimmy." He waited for a response. Moments later...

"Yes, Jimmy, I can hear you," he replied. "I'm afraid that I am in a bad place. I don't think that I can stand up right now."

"It's okay," he said, trying to sound confident. We have come to rescue you. Zoonee and Ryan are on their way to get Ori. When he gets here, we will get you outta here, okay? Hang in there," he encouraged.

"Thank you. I will try," said Pazou. Jimmy knew that their situation was dire, and they didn't have much time. He didn't know when Gorlev would be back, but he believed that, when he returned to him, he would require a definitive answer to his query. Jimmy believed that his part in this mission could be coming to an end.

He was forced to drink some of the water in his bucket, and wondered if they had given Pazou any to drink.

He called out to him:

"Pazou! Do you have water?" he asked.

"Yes, some, thank you for asking, Jimmy," he retorted. Jimmy decided to look through the hay on the cement floor to see if he could find something to free himself and Pazou. He tried one corner and then another. He did find a few bones of which Gorlev had spoken, but he didn't touch them. He tried another corner. There was some moon light coming in from a small crevice. It seemed to be a small, manmade hole, but it wasn't large enough for anyone to crawl through. Jimmy lay flat on his stomach and tried to see how far his arm would go through the hole to the other side. Whoever had dug the hole had been able to fit his arm all the way through it, and; perhaps, call for help.

Jimmy stretched his arm as far as it could go. His shoulder lodged itself inside the rocky portion of the hole, and it was cutting through his shoulder.

"Ouch!" he yelped. It was stuck snuggly--a perfect, yet unfortunate fit--and he was afraid to pull on it. He was afraid the wound in his shoulder would get worse, tearing deeper into his flesh. He lay there; his head vertical against the cold, rock wall, the smell of the dead filling his nostrils, afraid that he would soon become one of them.

About an hour or so had passed, and Jimmy had stopped his struggled to free himself. His only hope was that Gorlev, or one of his men would come with food and free him. He began to think of his father and mother. *How would they respond to his disappearance?* Surely, at some point, time would catch up to them, and they would know.

Several minutes later, Jimmy felt a tug on his hand. It was coming from outside the cell.

"Jimmy, Jimmy," a voice whispered. "It's Ori. I am here." Jimmy relieved to hear his voice.

"Ori, I'm stuck," he whispered. "I can't move, and Pazou is in the cell across from me. He can't walk," he said quickly.

"It's okay...," he said calmly. "I'm going to dig you out, until I can bust the rock. You need to stay still, okay?"

"Okay," Jimmy responded.

Minutes later Jimmy could hear, not only Ori, but Ryan, Zoonee, and Parelo.

Crack! Crack!

Jimmy's arm had been freed, and light was emanating from Ori's cane through the large hole in the rock. All Jimmy could do was lay his head down. Ori grabbed Jimmy by both arms and slowly dragged him out through the hole. Parelo and Ryan helped Jimmy to his feet, and they fled to the portal where they waited for Zoonee and Ori to return.

Ryan turned to Jimmy.

"You okay, man?" he asked, relieved to see that his friend was still alive.

"No, not really," Jimmy said, but managed a small grin. "He has my ring, too." Ryan looked at him and then back to the house. Ori and Zoonee were now inside Jimmy's cell. A few moments later, Zoonee, Pazou, and Ori came out of the hole. Ori placed Pazou's arm around his shoulder and slowly walked him down to the portal as Zoonee flanked them, watching out for trouble. For some reason, no one came out of the house or the barn. They were able to make it to the portal. Once they reached it, Ori repeated the words, and they were gone.

Jimmy woke up on a pallet in the floor between Ryan and Parelo. He could hear talking coming from the only bedroom in the cabin. He decided to join them. When he opened the door, he could see Zoonee on one side of the bed and Ori on the other. Ori got to his feet and led Jimmy out of the room and out of the cabin onto the porch. He could tell it was urgent.

"Jimmy, we have to go back to the house. I could tell that the ring was there, and I don't believe Gorlev was present. He does have men on the inside. He may have ordered them not to leave the house under any circumstances. That would explain why they didn't come out to stop us: They are guarding the rings. This may be our only opportunity to get them back," he explained. Jimmy couldn't believe what he was about to say. He was traumatized by the experience, but he knew Ori was right; he knew that he had to return for his ring.

They went back inside, and Ori gathered the boys around him. The boys reluctantly agreed to the risky idea; but they, too, knew that it might be their only chance. Ori moved in the bedroom quietly to speak to Zoonee.

"Zoonee, the boys and I are returning to Germany to the house. I believe that Gorlev is away and that he has left a small contingent of men to guard the rings, which is why we all got away unharmed," he elaborated. "I think you need to stay here with Pazou. We will return as soon as we have the rings in our possession." He placed his right hand on her left shoulder and looked over at Pazou. Zoonee had to numb portions of his body to free him from pain, and she used Ori's medicinal herbs to treat his other symptoms.

Zoonee nodded. She wanted to go, but she knew that Pazou needed her more. Ori quickly moved to the hearth and motioned for the boys to follow.

Once they were back in Germany, they moved swiftly to the house. They knew that the guards could spot them from the windows, but they didn't care. They used the hole in the cell to crawl into the house, one by one. Ori opened the cell door and they made their way up the stairs to the first story of the three-story structure.

Ori reached out to open the door at the top of the stairs. As he did, the door swung open, and they were all staring down the long end of an automatic rifle. Ori took a deep breath; no one moved. Then a figure came out of the shadows to pull on a string for light overhead. It was the blonde soldier. He recognized Ori and the boys and smiled at them.

"Need a little help?" he asked, lowering his weapon. "I will help you, if you will help me," he promised, as he offered his hand to Ori. Astonished, but relieved, by the soldier's actions, Ori shook his hand, and the solider led them through the kitchen of the house. The boys observed that another soldier seemed to be passed out in a chair at the kitchen table.

"Don't worry," he began, "I took care of him." When they reached the stairs that led to the next level, the man stopped. "Only one of you can go with me, now. If all of you go, then the guards on the second level will know that I am helping you."

"Why are you helping us, man?" Ryan asked. The man pointed to the left side of his face were Gorlev had burned it for his failure in the first battle.

"Because some leaders don't *value* the sacrifices of their men," he answered, glancing into Ori's eyes. They all immediately understood.

"I will go," said Ori. "The rest of you should wait outside—but don't be seen. Understand?" They all nodded and turned to leave the house. "Continue, my friend." The blonde soldier led Ori up the second flight of stairs. There were three doors. The blonde man held his finger to his mouth to signal Ori not to speak.

As they continued up the third flight of stairs, Ori looked back and could see shadows of feet moving under one of the doors, but no one opened it. When they had reached the third level, the man led him down a yellow hall to a white door on the left side. He stopped halfway to the door.

"These men are only allowed to come out a few times a day to relieve themselves. This is your way into your rings, which I assume is why you came," he whispered. Ori made eye contact with the blonde soldier and nodded his head. "When the door opens, you must disarm the men yourself. When this happens the other two guards will come out of the room down stairs. I will handle them. Okay?" he asked quietly. Again, Ori nodded, and they continued down the hall to the white door on the left.

The blonde soldier knocked on the door: "Okay, it is time for you to take your break, privates," he ordered. Ori could see that the blonde soldier was a sergeant in Gorlev's outfit. Ori could hear them shuffle their feet to the door. The blonde soldier moved down the hallway and aimed his gun toward the stairs.

As the door opened, Ori stepped in swiftly and hit the first soldier in the right side of his head, knocking him down. Before the next soldier could raise his gun, Ori twirled his staff back to the left and hit him in the side of the head, knocking him to the floor. As expected, the men heard the bodies of the privates hit the floor, and they came running up the stairs.

Bang! Bang! Bang!

The bullets from the blonde soldier's rifle rained down upon them, hitting one of them and causing him to fall over the rail to the first level. The firing continued from the blonde soldier and the second one.

Ori saw a locked box on the center of a desk. He ran to the box, grabbed it, and looked up at his only means of escape: a large square window behind the desk. He looked back, but the firing hadn't stopped. He looked forward and ran for the desk. He leaped on the desk and out the third story window with the box of rings under his arm.

Crash!

The window shattered, as Ori jumped through it. As he was falling, the boys ran to the side of the house to behold the spectacle. Ori, using his free arm to spin the staff at an unbelievable rate, was able to slow himself down to land on one knee.

The boys met him with large eyes and mouths agape. They couldn't believe what they had just witnessed. Ori dropped the box and broke the lock. He tossed Jimmy his ring, and he tossed Parelo his. They each placed the ring on their fingers respectively.

"Let's get out of here, guys," Ryan shouted. The boys turned to flee for the portal. But, Ori, pausing, looked back at the house.

"No!" he asserted. "I must keep my word. He helped us, and he saved us. I will *not* leave him."

Parelo, angry, but excited,

"Stand back!" he commanded. They all backed away from him. His eyes and his body began to glow a bright green, even his mouth was glowing.

"Ahhhhhhh!" he yelled. He threw up both his arms and his hands made fists in the air before him. A wave seemed to split the earth in front of him and the old, white house began to crack in the middle, just above the split Parelo had created. The foundation of the house caved in and began to fall into the deep chasm. The first, second, and third level cracked. The windows burst; the face of the house crumbled, and the blonde soldier could now be seen hanging from a window ledge.

Jimmy acted quickly. He held out his arms as Parelo had, and his eyes, body, and mouth began to glow a bright blue. Water appeared under the man, and it surrounded him in a ball. The soldier screamed as he fell into the safety of the ball water, which Jimmy brought slowly down to the grass in front of him. He laid the man down gently, and the water dissipated.

Ori came over to help the man up off the ground.

"Are you alright?" he asked, concerned. The man took Ori's hand, and Ori lifted him to his feet.

"Yes, thank you. That was amazing," he grinned, turning to Jimmy.

"Where can we take you?" Ori asked.

"I'm going home," he said. "I have no family, but I have friends here. If you can, take me to another part of Germany," he requested.

"Done." Ori smiled and extended his hand to the man. "What is your name?"

"My name is Gottfreid."

"It is nice to meet you, Gottfreid," Ori replied. "I will attempt to focus on another area of Germany at the portal. But, the truth is, I only know of one other place."

"That will be fine. I just need to get out of here. I will find my way home."

They went to the portal, and Ori recited the words.

Chapter Thirteen
The Stress Test

It was dawn...

A few moments later, they arrived at another portal in Germany. They were in a vast field and could see a small, yellow house, cattle, and a road several yards away. They all thanked Gottfreid. Gottfreid shook hands with them all.

"*Danke mein Freund*," he said to Ori, and he turned to walk toward the road.

"What'd he say?" asked Ryan.

"He said, 'Thank you, my friend,' Ori answered.

"I didn't know you spoke German, Ori," said Jimmy, looking over at Ori.

"There's still a lot about me that you don't know, Jimmy," replied Ori, watching the German solider walk away.

Ori turned to see the ancient posts and a frozen stream behind them, and he remembered that they needed to get back to his cabin to check on Pazou and Zoonee. He walked toward the portal with the boys, and they teleported home.

When they arrived, they each breathed a sigh of relief and hugged each other. Ori moved from the hearth to the bedroom door and knocked gently.

"Zoonee, we are back and safe," he said. Zoonee opened the door slowly and came into the front room to join them.

"Hi, guys," she began. "Pazou is sleeping. He is very weak, and he hasn't spoken in a while." She shifted her focus. "How did it go?" She looked at Ori and then to Jimmy. Jimmy held out his ring.

"We got our rings back," interrupted Parelo. "Sorry, go ahead, Jimmy."

"Yeah, but we had a little help," he admitted.

Zoonee made soup from what she could find in Ori's cabin, and they all sat down at his table to eat and to relay what had happened in Germany. They spoke of the soldier's kindness, of Ori's heroic leap, and of Parelo's phenomenal exhibition of power.

Zoonee, turning to Ryan,

"And what about you?" she asked. Ryan grinned at her.

"I was the moral support," he retorted. Everyone patted Ryan on the back and chuckled at his comment. "But I did rescue Pazou's staff and cane, along with my own. I found all of it in the barn," he proudly stated.

After dinner, Ori went out on the porch of his cabin, and Jimmy decided to join him. Ori turned to greet him.

"I was expecting you to come out here to worry with me. That's what a leader would do," he said, leaning on the rail of his wooden porch. Jimmy walked over to lean on it with him.

"I just wanted to thank you for saving my life," he said. "I am ashamed to admit that I was afraid to die." Ori squinted his eyes at him.

"We have all been afraid to die, Jimmy," he said. "That doesn't make you any less of a leader. Even though you were afraid, you showed great courage in risking your life for your friends: That makes you a great leader," he asserted, placing his right hand on his left shoulder. "There's no shame in that."

This made Jimmy feel better about himself. But, he had another question for Ori.

"What are we going to do next?" he asked, turning toward Ori.

Ori, sighing,

"I think we should rest—but not for long this time. Gorlev will not be pleased when he finds out what has transpired. He is most likely in Asia, searching for the Ring Bearer of the Silver Ring of Prophecy. If he finds him or her before us, then he will know our every move before we make it. Once this happens," he paused, "Defeating him will be impractical. We will have no choice, but to run from him—or accept defeat."

"Then we must find him *first*," Jimmy stated.

"Yes, we *must*," Ori emphasized. "But, for now, you and Ryan need to go home to your families and rest for a couple of days. Pazou won't be able to make the trip, so Zoonee must stay here to care for him." Jimmy nodded in agreement. It made him feel better to know that Zoonee would be out of harm's way, and he went in to get Ryan and to say goodbye to Zoonee. The two of them placed their powerful gifts back into Ori's chest for safekeeping.

When Jimmy and Ryan returned to the house, they discussed the group's next big objective. As Ori had done, Jimmy emphasized how critical it was for them to get to the Ring Bearer first.

"What's he or *she* called again?" asked Ryan. "The Silver Ring of *what*?"

"*Prophecy*," retorted Jimmy.

"So, his or *her* power is to foretell the coming of *someone* or *something*?" he queried.

"I think it's more general than that," Jimmy responded. "According to Ori, this Ring Bearer can see the future. But, yeah, he or *she* can do that, too."

"That doesn't sound so bad," he said. Jimmy turned to glance at him, puzzled by his remark. "I mean," he began, as he pushed buttons on his controller, "*He* or *she* could shoot laser beams from *his* or *her* eye sockets," he grinned.

"Go to bed," Jimmy said, throwing a Star Tale's pillow at his head.

"I'm just sayin'," Ryan replied, turning off his video game console and pulling the covers up over his body.

The next morning, Ryan and Jimmy awoke and could hear voices coming from Ryan's kitchen. They both looked over at each other, and they realized that Jimmy's parents had come to pick him up and to visit with Ryan's mother.

They both made it to their feet, and Jimmy grabbed his bag of clothes and supplies, realizing that he still hadn't used any item from the bag. He crept down the hallway to eavesdrop on the conversation to make sure that he was prepared for questioning.

Once he felt like it was safe, he walked into the kitchen. His mother and father were having coffee and doughnuts with Ryan's mother. Ryan, who had come into the kitchen earlier, was hovering down some chocolate ones. He quit for a moment when he saw Jimmy and grinned at him with chocolate teeth.

"Hey, Jim," his father said, being the first to greet him. "You ready to watch the game?"

"Yeah, ready," he responded, heading to the bathroom with his bag to shower. As he placed his duffle bag down on the white tile, he looked up in the mirror at himself. Normally, he focused on his appearance, but now he was looking inward, trying to decide if he recognized the person staring back him.

He wondered how Ryan was able to cope with so much change and pressure and still be his usual humorous, teenage self. His seemingly innocuous adventure had become a life-altering reality, and he was having some trouble staying in control of his feelings. He took his shower, and then he met his parents in the living room where they were saying goodbye to Ryan and his mother.

"Thanks for inviting us for breakfast," said Jimmy's mother.

"Oh, you're welcome. See you at work Monday," Ryan's mother replied. Jimmy walked outside and on to the porch.

"Aren't you going to say goodbye?" asked his father, sensing that something was amiss. Jimmy turned around to wave at Ryan and his mother before stepping into his Mom's car.

On the way home, it was quiet. Jimmy's father kept looking in his rearview mirror to check on him.

"You alright today, Son?" he asked, concerned. Jimmy lifted his head and nodded, but his father was not convinced. Jimmy knew he couldn't tell his father about his bruise on his head from the butt of rifle. He also knew he couldn't tell him about the gods, the rings, or Zoonee.

Jimmy didn't talk at all during the game, and his father kept looking over at him, wondering what was wrong. Jimmy's mind was in knots, and he didn't know how to untie it. His thoughts kept switching from the cell, to Zoonee, to his family, and then back to Gorlev. He had never experienced anything so terrifying or so hopeless as his brief stay in the cell. Nor had he ever been in love. His family had never meant more to him than they did now, and Gorlev was certainly going to pay for his transgressions.

Later that afternoon, as they both worked on two separate computers, his father decided to try one last time.

"You know, if you ever need to talk about anything, I'm here, and I won't judge you," he promised. Jimmy put down the multimeter that he was using to test the voltage of a power supply, and he began to cry softy. His father put down his screw driver and came over to him. Jimmy turned into his arms, and his father held his head against his broad chest. He didn't say anything; he just held him, trying to hold back his own tears for his son.

After a few minutes, Jimmy sniffed and unclenched his arms from his father's waist.

"I'm just dealing with a lot of teenager stuff right now," he said, looking down at the concrete floor of the garage. Jimmy's father put his hand on his head.

"I understand. It's okay," he replied, feeling a little better about his son. "I went through the same stuff when I was a teenager." Jimmy smiled at this response. He knew--for once--his father had never gone through what he was going through. His father caught his smile, and reciprocated with one of his own and rubbed his head one more time.

"Ouch!" Jimmy responded. *Uh-Oh*, he thought. His father leaned over to have a look at his head.

"Dang, Son, what did you do to your head?"

"I...was swinging from a vine in the woods by Ryan's house, and it sort of broke...and I sort of hit my head on the ground," he lied. His father examined it a little more.

"Why the hell didn't you tell Ms. Trigee? She's a nurse," he said, waiting for a response. *Ori had already put some medication on it at his cabin, but it left a bruise—and it still hurt*, Jimmy reflected.

197

"I...don't know," he said, as his father looked at him, confused.

"Well, have your mother look at it when you go inside," he retorted. "You okay, though?" he checked.

"Yeah, I'm good now, Dad. Thanks," he said, turning to finish working on the computer.

He did feel better, even though he couldn't divulge the whole truth. He was glad that his father hadn't left him alone this time. His father normally chose not to pry, but to let Jimmy come to him when needed.

That night, as Jimmy lay in bed, he replayed the last few days in his mind. He began to try to formulate a plan that would bring all this to an end. The only strategy they hadn't tried, thus far, was to take the fight to Gorlev himself. Gorlev was always one step ahead of them, and he wasn't sure why. He believed that they were always on the defensive; but, at some point, they would have to launch their own attack.

After contemplating a strategy to defeat Gorlev, he looked above him at the May Sting poster. He imagined superimposing Zoonee's face for May Sting's, and he also imagined what it would be like to be married to her and to have kids. He knew he wasn't ready for marriage or fatherhood, but he indulged his imagination. He couldn't visualize them living in Antarctica, but he could see them living together in Newford. He also believed that his father would be proud of him for finding a "go-getter," as he called them.

After this, he thought of his parents. He had never had a reason to miss them, until now, and he had never felt closer to his father. His mother had usually cared for him and provided for him, but now his father had become more relevant and necessary to his life. He was determined to continue this mission, and he would not let them down.

Chapter Fourteen
The Next Step

It was Monday afternoon. Jimmy's mother had already dropped him off at Ryan's to finish up on their science project. Jimmy and Ryan were walking up to Ori's cabin with their backpacks full of necessities. They both hoped that there would be better facilities where they were headed, but they didn't expect it.

Parelo opened the door for them, and he and Ori greeted them both.

"*Ola, mi amigos*," he said, standing aside so Jimmy and Ryan could walk into the cabin. They sat their heavy bags down on the floor.

Ori smiled.

"Prepared, gentlemen?" he asked.

Ryan, grinning at Ori,

"Yeah, I brought *five* pairs of underwear," he bragged, as everyone chuckled. Zoonee, overhearing them, came out of the bedroom.

"Hey, Zoonee," Jimmy began, "How is Pazou?"

"He's a little better today, but it will take some time for him to heal," she said, looking around at everyone.

"He's strong," Parelo replied. "He will be okay."

"Yeah, he will," said Ryan, grinning, attempting to reassure her and to cheer her up.

"Can I talk to you outside?" Jimmy asked her. Zoonee looked up at him and nodded her head. She followed him outside, as the others watched, smiling at the young couple.

Once outside and out of ear range, Jimmy took Zoonee's left hand.

"I don't know what's happening with us," he said, looking into her dark eyes. "I do know that I care a lot about you, and I don't want to see you get hurt."

Zoonee, beaming,

"I don't know either, but I care about you, too," she replied, taking his other hand. This comment made Jimmy feel very happy.

"If I don't make it back--," he began.

"You *better*," she threatened, forcing a smile from him. He reached out for her, and they hugged each other, as Parelo and Ryan stood by the window, grinning at both of them.

When they entered the cabin, Parelo stepped in front of Zoonee.

"Don't worry...," he paused for a moment. "I'll bring him back to you, Little Sister." He reached out and hugged her.

"Yeah, we won't let anything happen to this *dork*," Ryan jested, punching Jimmy in his right arm. "Just so long as he doesn't go runnin' off, again, trying to be the heroin." Everyone laughed.

"I think you mean *hero*, Ryan," Ori corrected.

Ori turned to Jimmy. "But, he is right, Jimmy. We have to work together as a team and only make sacrifices when they are necessary. Understand?" Jimmy understood and agreed with Ori in principle, but he wasn't going to let anyone of them get hurt—if he could help it.

They all went in to see Pazou before leaving for Asia. He was asleep and alive. Zoonee had used her powers as best she could to facilitate his healing, but he was still in pain, and would take many days to heal. They each went over and patted his left hand or left arm, and Ori said a Greek prayer to Asclepius for healing.

Jimmy observed Ori's praying, and wondered why he had never felt compelled to pray to a god. His family wasn't very religious, so he guessed that was the reason. He had been to church a few times with his friends when he was younger, so he had assumed that there was a god. The idea of many gods, however, wasn't a topic that he had ever considered entertaining until recently. He didn't understand a word of what Ori was saying, but he got the gist of it, and he knew that it was for Pazou.

After Ori had finished, they all walked over to Ori's wooden chest. Jimmy put on his ring; Ryan picked up his staff and cane, and Parelo made a fist and kissed his ring. Ori stood quietly with his eyes closed for a few moments and then spoke:

"Let's go, gentlemen. Time to save the planet," he said, resolutely.

"No more, Mr. Nice Teenager," Ryan said, looking side-to-side at all of them.

Ori twirled his staff into position.

"In the name of the gods, give us Guardians passage!"

www.ingramcontent.com/pod-product-compliance
Lightning Source LLC
Chambersburg PA
CBHW020239130626
46549CB00005B/1973